DOW
MONSTER
HOLE

or

Don't Be Afraid, I Am Only a Child

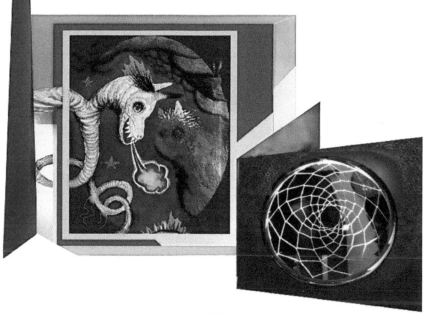

Story & Illustrations

Carmela Tal Baron

DOWN THE MONSTER HOLE or Don't Be Afraid, I Am Only a Child
Story and illustrations by: Carmela Tal Baron
All Copyrights reserved © 2019 by Carmela Tal Baron
Published in the United States by:
Designs for Enlightenment - Turtle Island
Contact: tal.carmela@gmail.com
ISBN: 9780578510781   1. Juvenile Fiction - Monsters
2. Juvenile Fiction - Action & Adventure
3. Juvenile Fiction - Imagination & Play

TURTLE
ISLAND

Designs for Enlightenment

Author's Note

I n **DOWN THE MONSTER HOLE** or *Don't Be Afraid I'm Only a Child,* a child's journey through a fictional maze full of wonders and challenges turns into a mind-expanding search for meaning.

Tom, a runaway, clashes with a gang of wicked clocks and loses his way and his sense of time. After wandering around and making new friends, Tom finds himself alone in a cemetery for machines. There, amid the junk of the mechanical remains, he discovers a hidden kingdom of monsters and puzzles, which peak his curiosity. As Tom travels from adventure to adventure and from one challenge to another, clues to the meaning of his quest unfold. At last, he meets Seven, a pretty flower-maiden, in a magical garden.

Seven and her flowery maidens cheer Tom up with their early morning chanting in motion. They brighten his journey with a spark of enlightenment and good advice. At the end of the maze, he learns that who and what he imagined the "King of All Monsters" to be is none other than a representative of law and order. Tom also realizes that if one wishes to find his way through the "Law and Order" maze, he must first master his own skills of self-discipline. This realization helps Tom find his way to the world where he belongs and his path back home.

Contents

CHAPTER 1

Tom's Battle with the Clocks

This is a story about a young boy named Tom who had a great fondness for sleeping. He would often get lost in his dreams and have a hard time waking up.

He lived with his parents and baby sister in a small fishing village somewhere along the northern seashore. The hardworking residents of this village would compete with the sun to see who could rise earlier in the morning. They always won.

Tom was different from the other villagers. He relished his sleep. The bright rays of the sun could not breach the dark tunnel where a caravan of dreams took him for magnificent rides. Even the high-pitched cries of his baby sister could not wake him up.

Tom's father, a collector of clocks, had a grandfather clock with a pendulum. The clock featured a little clown that would appear to perform his gymnastics whenever the clock rang. His father also had a cuckoo clock with a bird that flew out through an open door to sound a cuckoo call and then withdrew. Another clock featured a soldier that marched out as the clock struck the hour and dutifully returned inside.

Tom's father's wide array of clocks rivaled that of any other collector in the village.

One afternoon, while Tom's father, Hans, was busy cleaning and mending his clocks, he dreamt up a scheme: how to wake his sleepy son in the morning. That night, he placed three clocks near Tom's bed and set each one to a different time.

The next day, the alarm on the first clock, this one with the signs in Latin instead of numbers, rang at exactly a quarter to seven, waking up our sleeping hero. Annoyed, Tom opened his eyes and tried to remember his splendid dream so rudely interrupted. He turned onto his back and tried to fall asleep, eager to recapture his dream. But at seven o'clock precisely, the alarm on the second clock, this one with a sunny face, rang. Tom opened his eyes.

This ringing is ridiculous.

He closed his eyes again. Then, at a quarter past seven, the third alarm rang. Tom jumped out of his bed, unnerved, and said, "Not only did I not finish my dream, but, with all the ringing, I forgot what my dream was about!"

Every morning since, the three clocks rang, interrupting Tom's glorious chain of dreams. But now, at least, he always managed to wake up and get to school on time.

One morning, when our story truly begins, Tom awoke to the alarms but did something bold and unexpected. After the third ring had faded, he jumped out of his bed, wiped his eyes, yawned twice, picked up one of his wooden clogs, and smashed all three clocks at once. His mother, Alva, rushed into his room and saw the shattered clocks on the floor.

Startled, she called out, "Hans, oh Hans, come see! Your son has broken the clocks! What are we going to do with him?"

Hans walked into the room, surveyed the mess, and looked Tom in the face. "Little monster!" he said, his voice as cutting as glass and his face pink with anger, before abruptly leaving the room.

Chagrined, Tom got dressed and went to school without any breakfast.

Outside, the sun, round and majestic, rose and woke the drowsy flowers. Tom walked the green path to school, observing his surroundings.

The kind sun rouses the flowers so gently after the cold night, like a mother should wake up her children.

Beautiful butterflies cast in vivid hues rested on the petals of the opening flowers and luxuriously sipped their first drink of fresh nectar. Tom envied the butterflies feasting at the flower dishes, wishing he, too, could sip nectar for breakfast.

I'm eleven years old, and this morning I waged war for the first time. I faced a gang of noisy clocks, and I slew all three of them, all at once. I am thirsty, too!

Time is art.

CHAPTER 2

The Latecomer

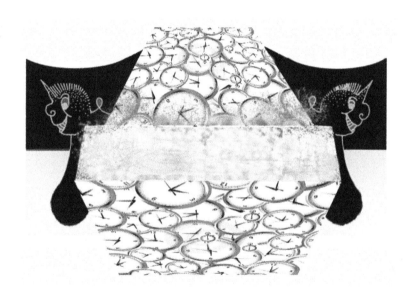

When Tom entered the classroom, all the students were already there. He tiptoed to his seat so as not to disturb the teacher who stood at the blackboard writing, her back to the class. But, the teacher heard him enter, and without turning around greeted him loudly, "GOOD MORNING, Tom." Even the pigeons on the windowsill stopped feeding their fledglings, lifted their beaks, and listened.

Heavy silence descended on the classroom. Then, a box full of pencils fell from one of the desks, and all the children looked in the direction of the sound. The pigeons resumed their feeding, and the teacher turned around and faced her class.

"She must have secret eyes in the back of her head," whispered Ram, Tom's best pal. Tom's heart lifted when he heard the familiar voice. But, before he could utter a sound, a stronger voice intruded: "Tom, did your father sign the letter I gave you the day before yesterday, the one about your habit of being late to school? And you, Danny," the teacher continued, pointing to the boy who had dropped his pencils, who was crawling under the desks, "Why do you always drop your books and pencils?"

"I forgot the letter," Tom said, blushing.

"It's because I'm unlucky," Danny said, getting up off the floor and placing his pencils, one by one, back into its box.

"Forgot again!" the teacher said as she approached Tom. "That's unacceptable. Go home and ask your father to sign that letter. I'll meet you outside the classroom door."

Tom collected his books and walked out of the classroom, embarrassed.

Why does everyone like to pick on me? I'm not welcome here. I'm not welcome at home, either, with Dad mad at me for smashing his clocks into pieces, and Mom preoccupied with my baby sister. Oh boy! It was reckless of me to smash the poor clocks. Where can I go now? I have no clue. Anywhere but home!

There were no children in the schoolyard except for Tom. As he walked out through the gate, he noticed two kittens fooling around with a ping-pong ball that someone had left behind.

CHAPTER 3

Tulips, Wild Flowers, & Adventures

Tom went for a walk. The fields were full of tulips arranged in a magnificent, colorful display—rows and rows of perfect blooms disappearing off into the horizon. It was early May, the beginning of the most beautiful time of the year.

On his way, Tom saw farmers working in the fields and fishermen mending their nets.

"Everyone is so hardworking, except me. I have nowhere to go because of wicked clocks and unsigned letters," Tom said to himself, kicking the dirt as he walked. But, as it was the month of May, the kindly sun did not allow children to linger on sad thoughts. Tom soon stopped worrying and just admired the beauty of the morning.

Suddenly, Tom came upon a bunch of carefree kids who had decorated themselves with garlands of wildflowers and tulips. Some kids ran barefoot; others wore sandals. His own wooden clogs felt too heavy. He wished he could take them off and run barefoot like these playful kids. He watched them intently as they frolicked near one of the canals, which crisscrossed that small fishing village along the northern seashore.

The kids were making colorful paper boats out

of pages of old magazines and launching them onto the flowing water of the canal. Tom recognized them as the children of the caravan-dwellers. They had appeared from nowhere the summer before and had since been stationed nearby.

Tom admired their freedom.

Perhaps it's fun to be a carefree caravan-dweller. If you don't like one kind of schooling, you may choose to learn another way. With them, I could wander around the land, learning to look and see things in a fresh way. The caravan-dwellers travel from one location to another. They might take me along, if I ask politely.

He plucked out the middle page from his school math book and folded it into a boat. Tom's boat rivaled those of the other kids as he dropped it into the canal, and it collided with the paper boat of a boy who looked like he was the leader of the caravan-dwelling kids. The kid raised his eyes from the two boats and saw Tom.

"Hey pal, welcome," the boy greeted Tom. "My name is Ian! What's yours?" he asked, extending his arm in a gesture of goodwill. "Would you like to join us after this game?" Ian called out to the others, "Looks like we have another kid to play with!"

"I am Tom. And yes, I would love to join you!"

As he spoke, he gave Ian a high five.

Tom folded yet another boat. This time, he pulled out a double sheet of paper from the middle of his calligraphy book.

Oh boy, is this adventure for real? Would they really take me along?

Elated, he launched his new boat toward the little pier where all the other boats were gathered.

When the children got tired of racing paper boats, they all boarded a rowboat moored to one of the piers in the canal. Ian stood front and center to make an announcement.

"Now we all are taking off in the direction of the graveyard for machines. Are you all ready?"

The kids whistled and cheered, "Hip hip hooray—to the graveyard! Off we go!" as they pushed the rowboat away from the pier and joined the stream, moving forward.

"Graveyard for machines?" Tom asked.

"Yes," Ian explained. "When a person passes away from this world, relatives bury their beloveds in a graveyard. But what do you do if the heart of an engine stops beating because of old age or an accident?"

"You drag it to a graveyard for machines," Tom leapt to answer.

"We are caravan-dwellers," Ian said. "We live in trailers or vans. Now, we are parked near this graveyard. During the day, those among us work and fix those machines that still have a chance to come alive. At night, we gather around the campfire, dancing and singing, including us kids. Often, the adults even allow us to stay up late into the night."

When the rowboat reached its destination, the graveyard for machines was visible in the distance. The kids jumped onto the pier. Ian turned to Tom. "Would you like to visit us?"

Ian's parents and his little sister lived in a double-decker bus that was painted crimson with light-blue stripes. Ian explained that once it had been an ordinary bus carrying passengers to their destinations. Now it was a mobile home. On the bottom level, Ian's parents had their bedroom and a kitchen. Upstairs were the kids' rooms and a storage space. The roof was covered with green edible plants, cooling the house in summertime and keeping it warm in the cold season.

Not far from their caravan, amid the elm trees, Ian's father, Robin, was playing his guitar. When he noticed the kids, he struck a few chords from a song he called "Story Time."

Ian told Tom that he was happy to see his father back for a break from his work and that his father loved sharing, in song, stories about great travelers. The kids gathered around, listening to a ballad that Robin told them he had composed about Vasco da Gama, who had sailed from Portugal to India centuries ago.

Tom drew a moral from the story.

Great explorers are never forgotten.

Ian's mother, Mel, offered the kids a basket full of freshly baked cinnamon muffins.

While enjoying his favorite cinnamon-vanilla flavor, Tom noticed a round object with feathers attached to it hanging near the window of this colorful, adorable mobile home.

"What is the net-like object in the window?" Tom asked, pointing toward the caravan.

"This is a dream catcher," replied Ian's mother, who loved doing craftwork as well as collecting special designs.

"A dream catcher?" Tom repeated after her.

"Yes," she assured him. "This wooden ring holds the boundaries of a net woven with the intention to catch dreams."

"How does it work?" he wondered, admiring the craft of the woven design.

"Well, the net allows the good dreams to pass through the center while the bad dreams get stuck in the margins, hoping for attention before they vanish at dawn!"

"It sounds so useful; how did you learn about it?" Tom asked with curiosity.

"It came into our possession when Robin's father exchanged goods with a far-land native, known also as a medicine man, who sailed all the way from New Amsterdam across the Atlantic Ocean many years ago!"

Mel loved sharing tales, and Tom lit up with excitement. "A catcher of dreams! I'd love to try one, one day!"

"Storytime has ended!" announced Ian. Gesturing to Tom, he turned and walked on. The kids, including Tom, followed him.

In the center of the machine graveyard stood an old windmill surrounded by all kinds of dusty machines and cars—tall cranes, an old tank, a locomotive engine with five train cars attached to it, an old cement mixer, and many bicycles. There was also a huge pile of cell phones, a mountain of computers, even some old airplanes and helicopters—all collected in this magnificent wasteland!

The children played hide-and-seek and cops-and-robbers all through that afternoon. When the day ended, Ian said, "Well, we have to go home. Tom, would you like to visit us tomorrow?"

"Yes, yes, I sure would," Tom agreed eagerly.

"Bye-bye, then," waved the kids.

CHAPTER 4

Is It a Hippo, or Is It a Rhino?

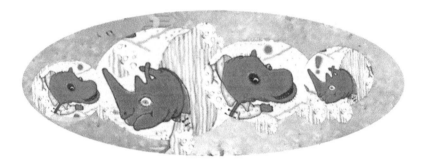

Tom found himself alone in the graveyard of machines.

It's time to return home, but the letter is not signed, those clocks are still broken, and my father is so very strict.

Suddenly, something moved. It made a creaking sound that reminded Tom of an old man groaning. At first alarmed, Tom turned and realized that it was only the old windmill moving on its own.

Darkness rested on the wings of the windmill, and, far away, a campfire glowed.

That is probably the campfire of the caravan-dwellers.

Tom wondered if Ian, his new friend, might be watching the same campfire from his place!

Was he awake, too? Would he ever see the caravan-dwelling kids again?

Tom followed the winding staircase up the windmill and looked out the narrow window. It was windy, and Tom shivered. Then he saw a large hippopotamus lying on the ground below.

"What is a hippo doing here?" Tom wondered, opening his eyes wide in disbelief. "That couldn't be a hippo; perhaps it's a rhino."

20

"Eek, eek, eek," the old windmill said, taking advantage of the breeze to do some night exercises. He ran down the narrow staircase and crept towards the mysterious beast only dimly visible in the dark.

Tom inched closer.

This strange animal is not moving at all. Perhaps he or she's in deep sleep.

Once again, the wind blew, a bit colder than before, and the wings of the windmill began groaning, as if in pain, frightening Tom.

Tom ran away from the sound without knowing why or where he was heading. The graveyard was so vast that Tom forgot where the exit was. He came to a halt, confused. While standing there, he reasoned out loud, "I must know whether I saw a hippo or a rhino." He carefully and quietly retraced his steps back to the enormous animal. But three steps away from it, he tripped on a stone and tumbled into the open mouth of the beast.

Tom was afraid to open his eyes.

Now, I'm a goner.

He mumbled to himself, and, encouraged by the sound of his own voice, opened one eye. "For the first time in my life, I'm dying."

The animal's jaws had stayed open, and Tom could feel the night air wafting into its mouth.

Strange animal.

Gathering his nerve, he crawled out of its mouth.

It was then that Tom realized that what he had thought was a beast was only an old junked car with its hood open. Tom sighed in relief and sat down to rest at the foot of the old wreck he affectionately nicknamed "Hippo."

Exhausted from all the excitement, Tom fell asleep in no time. Because it was a chilly night, he woke up after a few minutes to look for a warmer spot. He decided it would be safe to get inside Hippo's mouth to sleep.

While still dozing, Tom saw through the slits of his half-closed eyes another monster slowly approaching. The strange monster opened its mouth and spoke in a rusty voice, "Goodnight, Hippo, it's time to wake up. The carnival is about to start."

"A very good night to you too, sweet Rhino," Hippo answered. "Is it already time to wake up?"

Tom was confused, and he asked himself,

Why is Rhino wishing Hippo good night if it is time to wake up?

"Not only do you need to wake up, you have to change out of your pajamas and wear something dressy for the night."

"What are you going to wear?" Rhino asked.

"I will wear a white bow tie and a triangular military hat. In that, I should look very respectable," Hippo said, as he yawned.

"Hippo, Hippo," said Rhino, suddenly alarmed. "What is inside your mouth?"

"Inside my mouth? I have no idea. As a matter of fact, I do feel something in my throat."

Tom was listening attentively to this strange conversation. He pulled his legs close to his chest and pondered.

In the beginning, I suspected it was a hippo. Then, it seemed like a wrecked car. And now, it turns out I really am cradled between the huge jaws of a real hippo and before us stands a beastly rhino. Where am I? I must be losing my mind!

"I think some huge insect has found a home inside your mouth," Rhino suggested to Hippo. "If you cannot or do not want to close your mouth when you are asleep, you should at least remember to brush your teeth, so you don't have uninvited guests settling inside."

Tom jumped out of Hippo's mouth. Once on the ground, he shook his hands and feet of dust and said to his stunned audience, "Don't be afraid, I'm only a child."

Terrified, Rhino and Hippo galloped away. Tom laughed. Their heavy bodies looked funny as they were fleeing, making odd, rusty noises with each step they took.

CHAPTER 5

The Kingdom of Monsters Rises from a Daylong Nap

Tom ran toward the windmill and climbed up until he reached the small window at the top of the staircase. From there, he looked down at what was happening below. He could not spot the hippo-rhino pair. Instead, he was amazed to see a whole kingdom of monsters waking up, slowly rising from a daylong nap.

The old, rusty cranes gently elevated their long necks, lifted their heads, and turned into a gang of giraffes.

The tallest crane, with a head composed of three parts, turned into a dinosaur. Tom could not believe his eyes! How could it be the ancient and horrifying creature his teacher had told him about, which had walked the earth millions of years ago? The cement mixer on top of the old truck spun faster and faster. It looked like a giant hunchback with one huge eye, like the Cyclops Tom once saw in a fairytale book. Congregating near the Cyclops were three electric teapots that turned into a trio of ostriches.

The old fishing boats had dressed up like a band of sharks. But to Tom's astonishment, these were cheerful, smiling sharks.

Transformed into a colony of bats, the old,

junked airplanes had taken off and were hovering above. These mischievous bats stuck airline logos to their wings in honor of the good old days when they carried passengers across the sky.

When the helicopters turned into huge flies, they released a buzzing cloud of smoke almost as big as the monstrous bats themselves. A pile of old typewriters slowly transformed into big birds with yellow feathers, except for one very old-fashioned typewriter, which turned into a witch with a blue beard.

"Bluebeard is my name," the witch announced and hopped onto a tall vacuum cleaner that instantly changed into a handsome broom.

Two old computers were dressed up like a pair of robots. "Willing and Able are our names," they said in unison. They were shoving together a huge pile of cell phones that looked like many cells of one body. The little mountain they made gleamed like a cluster of crystal encircled by small dark stones.

The guests moved closer and stood nearby, gazing at the shining wonder. Many pairs of bicycles buzzed about the periphery of the circle, transforming into huge insects.

Tom's curiosity soared while witnessing the huge, colorful swarm. It was not the first time he'd seen insects. These were the very same insects he saw every day, only, until now, he had never paid close attention. (To tell the truth, insects used to scare Tom a bit.) He'd miss the beauty and magnificence of these colossal specimens. He strangely felt no fear, even though the insects' size and behavior were more than intimidating.

Tom made a vow to himself:

When I get out of here, I am going to pay close attention and never ignore even the smallest creature on Earth!

He stood motionless at the top of the windmill, as the monsters approached and slowly formed half a circle around it.

The Cyclops continued to roll his eyeball faster and faster, back and forth, left and right. The bats flapped their wings in a strange, haunting beat, reminding Tom of the old children's rhyme, "Row, row, row your boat."

And then Hippo approached, looking up at Tom, wearing a most elegant and magnificent outfit.

Hippo opened his already open mouth wider than before and exclaimed, "As a representative of the citizens of this kingdom, I request that you identify yourself!"

"I have already told you that I am only a child! " Tom replied in a faint voice that got lost in the big, dark night.

"What?" shouted Hippo, as he attached a special listening device to his left ear.

Tom cupped his hands around his mouth and called out at the top of his voice, "I am a child, and my name is Tom!"

"A child? What is a child?" the monsters groaned in low voices, talking and imploring each other in great wonder.

"A child… a child… a child is like a little man," Tom said, struggling for words, "only younger and smaller."

Animated, the monsters exclaimed in unison: "A human cub, a human cub!"

Hippo hushed the excitable monsters and asked in an earnest voice, "Can a child also be a monster?"

"A child is a child, but a child can be a monster, too," Tom said. "This morning, for instance, my father called me a monster and he didn't mean it as a compliment! If he'd ever been to this kingdom of gentle and friendly monsters, he would have called me something else!" Tom concluded, pausing to see what his curious audience might think of that.

Hippo furrowed his brow as he attached a monocle to his right eye. He looked at Tom intently and signaled to his pals to gather around him for a brief consultation.

Plodding and stomping, leaving deep prints in the ground with each step, the monsters approached Hippo. Huge, red cockroaches emerged from their holes, waving their thin, blue antennae and calling out, "Listen everyone! A child, yes, a little one, has arrived in our kingdom!"

Hippo hushed the excited roaches, and the monsters huddled together for a long while. "We demand that you give yourself up, so we can study you more closely," the hippo announced, while wiping the sweat off his big, wide brow.

"I'm not sure," said Tom in a whiny voice.

"Why, are you scared of us?" asked the hippo in a polite but prideful voice.

"I am not afraid of you, but I must admit I am scared of the roaches, the red cockroaches down there!"

"Ha, ha, ha," the monsters burst into wild laughter. "He is not afraid of the monsters, but he is frightened of the red cockroaches."

The big, multi-legged caterpillar also exploded into high-pitched laughter and circled about. Round and round he went until he almost bit off his tail!

But the red cockroaches, insulted, bent their heads down, shedding tears that filled their footprints, turning them into tiny pools of grief. Tom felt shame, suddenly noticing how majestic the cockroaches truly were. Just about to ask for their forgiveness, he was interrupted.

"Total silence everyone!" commanded the hippo, motioning to the caterpillar to take all the red roaches out for a midnight ride around the graveyard.

The wet, red roaches jumped on top of the caterpillar. They wiped off their tears with their tender antennae and were all smiles when Tom waved goodbye to them.

The caterpillar vanished into the distance, blowing green puffs of smoke from his ears and rattling like a moving train as he lumbered on: Tar, TAR – Tar, TAR – Tar, TAR...

"Now, you can safely come down," Hippo called out to Tom, winking at Rhino. When Tom came down from the top of the windmill, Rhino sat him in a swing attached to the mouths of two tall giraffes. Thrilled, Tom swung back and forth, sounding Native American battle cries like in Wild West movies.

"Ahoy Ho Ahoy Ho Ahoy Ho...Now I understand why the giraffe's neck is so long, and why two giraffes are better than one. So, kids can swing and have the time of their lives!"

Tom laughed out loud.

CHAPTER 6

Nice to Meet You; My Name is Tom

Catching his breath, Tom saw all the monsters moving toward him. One by one they approached, gazing at him in wonder. Tom and the monsters stared at each other in a strange silence.

"May I introduce myself to you all?" Tom asked, pausing for a long moment before adding, "My name is Tom."

All at once, the monsters began talking and pointing at Tom.

"Attention, attention, your attention please!" Hippo raised his voice. "Everyone, please, take turns talking!"

Gurgle, the huge, old giraffe, swung his long neck around and declared, "What a short and useless neck this boy's got. Not even long enough to turn full circle and look behind his back, not to mention that he cannot tell what's happening at the top of a tree."

All the monsters, big and small, nodded in agreement. The hunchback Cyclops stepped forward next, rapidly turning his single big eye from left to right and back again, before commenting, "And what tiny little eyes. It's hard to believe he can see anything at all!"

Rhino, next in line, took off his checkered hat gracefully, scratched his front right leg with his horn, and speculated, "I have a sharp horn in the center of my forehead, and everyone respects me. But how can this tiny and helpless child protect himself?"

Tom wondered what his classmates would say if they knew animals looked at kids this way.

Come to think of it, kids always have something to say about animals, but a child can only guess what an animal thinks of him.

Suddenly the huge, multi-legged caterpillar returned from his night journey and circled around the child, halting Tom's thoughts. The caterpillar added his two cents:

"Only one pair of skinny, frail legs! Hard to believe this kid can run very far on those legs," said the caterpillar, laughing as green puffs of smoke came from his ears.

Again, the monsters loudly talked at once. Tom couldn't grasp what they were saying, but it was clear they were talking about him. In his heart, he knew their words shouldn't hurt him. He felt an odd combination of uneasy and confident, but he did not utter a word.

"Attention, attention, please!" Hippo scolded the noisy monsters again, trying to make an announcement: "Ear-El, the red cockroach, is requesting the right to speak."

Ear-El hopped on top of Rhino's horn, so that he could be seen and heard by all present, and said, "I think you are all wrong, not to mention your rude behavior!"

Again, all the monsters started talking at once, interrupting Ear-El.

"Attention, attention, please! Let Ear-El finish what he has to say," Hippo scolded the monsters once again, while asking Ear-El, "And what makes you think the monsters are so wrong in their judgment?"

Ear-El straightened his blue antennae, repositioned himself on Rhino's horn, and recited:

"The mighty elephant's trunk is very long,
but the rhino has just a tough little horn.
The Cyclops has one big eye to stare, and the
caterpillar many legs to spare.
The cockroach owns a pair of antennae
to sense around and scan new grounds.
And the butterfly sports a pair of wings
to fly and soar on gentle winds..."

"We already know all that!" growled the monster turtle.

"To make a long story short," continued Ear-El, "every animal is unique in some very special way."

"So what? So what?" the caterpillar asked, laughing.

"Which means that Tom, too, has some special quality unique to him!" Ear-El summed up his thoughts, feeling proud of his insight.

"And what is that special something that only he possesses?" Hippo asked the red cockroach.

"I don't know yet. I still have no clue," Ear-El blushed with some embarrassment, as he concluded his argument. "Tom is still new here. Let us get to know him first before we pass judgment!"

Tom was happily surprised upon listening to Ear-El, the red cockroach. Deep in his heart, he would have never believed that a huge, red cockroach would rise to his defense so heroically.

Smiling, Tom stood up, thanked Ear-El, and announced, "Now, I would like to tell you a story about a very famous caterpillar with one hundred legs."

"Does the story have a good ending?" asked one of the ostriches, hesitantly raising her head out of a pile of sand.

"We want a good ending. Otherwise, shall we break for tea?" suggested the other ostrich.

"We shall see when we get there," replied Tom, pausing briefly before starting his tale, "but first, let's start from the beginning:

Once upon a time, there was a slim and very agile caterpillar with one hundred legs. His name was Fly. All the animals and birds adored Fly and watched him with amazement whenever they saw the nimble caterpillar around the forest. Fly would always move all of his one hundred legs flawlessly and in perfect harmony, without the slightest misstep.

One day, a tiny caterpillar, also taken with Fly's beauty, said, 'How handsome you are, Fly, and how smart. And your skin is so smooth and brilliant!' Fly was not used to such compliments. In fact, he did not care for them. He just loved to run, so he was curt with the tiny caterpillar. 'What is it that you want, tiny caterpillar?'

'I have a question,' said the tiny caterpillar with much hesitation.

'Well, ask away, then,' said Fly.

'Tell me, Fly, what does your sixty-eighth leg do when your ninety-ninth leg is up and turning right?'

Fly laughed wholeheartedly and explained, 'It is very simple, very simple indeed, don't you get it? No? So, let me demonstrate.'

While Fly was trying to demonstrate, his legs got all tangled up and he collapsed. Fly was stunned but did not lose his composure. He smiled, a little bit embarrassed, and apologized for the unexpected mishap. His crowd of fans seemed confused, shuffling their legs but waiting patiently.

Fly recovered quickly. Getting up, he shook the grains of sand from his slim, elongated body, exhaled twice, and continued his demonstration, as if nothing had happened. Unfortunately, his legs got tangled up again and he couldn't move at all!

'What is happening to me?' he cried. 'When I don't think, my legs always move in perfect order. But when I start thinking and try to figure things out, I get all mixed up.'"

"That's what I have always been saying," interjected the ostrich, as she was digging in the sand. "There is no need to think too much!"

"You did not understand the story," said Ear-El, laughing.

"Attention, attention, please," Hippo hushed the crowed. "Save your remarks for the end!"

And Tom continued with his story.

"Fly's legs got so mixed up that no one could untangle them. The audience, led by the tiny caterpillar cadet, clapped and cheered in encouragement. But Fly bent his head down, refusing to be comforted or cheered up, or even to rise and stand up.

Fly, the renowned caterpillar with his one-hundred legs, continued to sit still on the ground, gazing nowhere, for days on end. Many days passed by, some even say years. His faithful friends from the forest, remembering his glorious past, took care of all his needs. But Fly, the champion runner, was sad. His useless, tangled legs grew thinner and weaker with every day that passed, and almost vanished."

Tom paused for a moment and looked at his audience, seeking a reaction to this shocking development.

The monsters looked at Tom in total silence, their mouths wide open. Extremely upset, the ostrich broke down in tears and cried. "What a sad and bitter ending! We want a story with a happy ending!"

"A happy ending, a happy ending, we all want a happy ending!" The monsters howled with disappointment.

Tom continued with his story.

"Fly, the legendary caterpillar known for his perfectly synchronized one hundred legs, was now totally grounded, sitting motionless and gazing into the horizon. He had been that way for days on end, days that turned into many moons.

One morning, Fly woke up from his sad sleep and discovered that his famous legs had totally disappeared! Fly looked at his long, smooth body with great astonishment. He didn't know if he should cry or rejoice. At any rate, he was bored with being stuck in one place all this time.

'A caterpillar without legs? Perhaps I am no longer a caterpillar; perhaps I am something else,' he mumbled to himself, while lifting his long body up and jumping on a low tree branch! He curled his body around the branch, and then leapt onto a higher branch and spiraled upward, moving from branch to branch, higher and higher, demonstrating with his smooth, legless body his newly found acrobatic skills.

'Ah! How good it feels now to be without

legs! What a surprise. If I still had my legs, they would most likely stand in the way of my acrobatic routine.'

The story of Fly spread throughout the forest. All the animals, birds, and insects would gather, whenever and wherever Fly could be found amusing himself, slipping with great ease from branch to branch, having fun being himself, practicing his new brand of flight to everyone's delight. From that day on, Fly the Runner became known as Fly the Flier, and in all the forest there was no better acrobat than Fly the Flier."

All the monsters broke into thunderous applause at the happy ending.

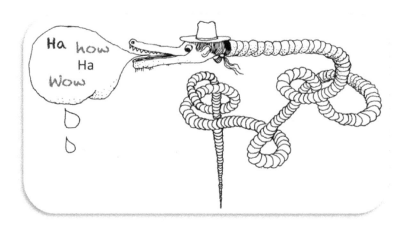

CHAPTER 7

Membership Rules
in the Kingdom of Monsters

"**Q**uiet, quiet, quiet, please!" Hippo stood up on his hind legs. "Before we go on with our evening program, I would like to ask Tom a question: tell me, please, how did you get here in the first place?"

"Ah... I don't know," Tom said, stuttering. "I was playing hide-and-seek, and it suddenly got dark, and I fell asleep. When I woke up, you all appeared."

"And what are you planning to do now?" Hippo asked.

"I wish I could take part in the Carnival of Monsters," said Tom politely.

All the monsters burst out laughing at the ridiculous thought.

"But you are not a monster, you've told us you're just a child," said Ear-El, the red cockroach.

Tom thought for a moment, then said with excitement, "I will disguise myself as a monster and make believe I am one, at least for tonight. Maybe one day, even you will believe me, as if I were a real monster! I don't think anyone is born a monster! Even you all were once only simple machines."

"And how are you going to dress up?" inquired Hippo.

"I will turn myself into a bat. I have always dreamed about flying at night."

"Cheers! Cheers! Cheers!" The bats in the crowd clapped their wings in unison.

"Are you familiar with the membership rules and regulations in our kingdom of monsters?" asked Rhino.

"No, I am not," said Tom. "Could you please explain them to me?"

Hippo stood up on his hind legs, straightened his tie, fixed his hat, and read out loud from a thick, dusty book entitled, *Membership Rules in the Kingdom of Monsters*:

"One. Only a remarkably ugly creature may be admitted. And the uglier, the better, as my grandfather, the prehistoric elephant, once advised," sighed Hippo, who was known to exaggerate about his magnificent past.

"Two. We also admit machines, automobiles, and various creatures who were damaged or injured in an accident, or became old, or were expelled from their native land, or fled because of danger.

"Three. Members are allowed to bother and annoy each other, but never ever to truly harm one another.

"Four. Members must stay awake from the end of sunset until the beginning of sunrise. Any member found asleep during nighttime will be expelled from this kingdom, without regard to that member's size or ugliness.

"Five. It is totally forbidden to tell anyone about our existence. Our kingdom is a secret, and we do not like strangers!

"However, for you, we will make an exception!" Hippo said to Tom. "Because you are already here and so earnest, we are willing to accept you as our honorary guest for this night only."

Hippo turned to Tom and asked him to place the palm of his hand on the Kingdom's book of membership rules. Tom put his hand on the dusty book and sneezed. Hippo lifted his front foot and laid it gently on Tom's head before coughing twice from the dust. Two sour-looking giraffes opened their mouths wide and blew out a shower of colorful confetti that landed on Tom's head.

All the monsters broke out in cheerful howls, and Hippo announced:

"From this moment on, you are a monster-in-training! The inaugural ceremony has come to an end."

CHAPTER 8

The Bizarre Rite of Blessings

Gurgle, the mighty giraffe, lifted his neck, stuck his head into a huge pile of clothing nearby, and, with a flourish, picked out a bat costume with his teeth, and gave it to Tom.

Tom put on his new outfit and flapped his new wings happily.

Out of nowhere, many bats appeared. They circled over Tom's head, and one bat, the darkest of them all, announced:

"The Rite of Blessings is about to begin!"

Hippo raised a golden wand, and, with a magic touch, transformed a group of old tanks into a band of elephants blowing trumpets!

Soon, cheerful military music sounded in the background.

One tank failed to enter into Hippo's magic circle in time and was left out. The red cockroaches covered it with a coat of flowers so it would still feel a part of the carnival.

Slowly and festively, the monsters approached Tom, and, one by one, they bestowed upon him their individual blessings.

Gurgle, the mighty and very talkative giraffe, licked Tom's nose and said, "My dear monster-in-training, may your neck stretch out longer and longer until you can see what the neighborhood kids are up to on the roof, and then tell the other kids waiting in the courtyard downstairs what you have seen."

Tom was baffled, but he nodded and smiled politely.

Gurgle arched his mighty, long neck downward and licked Tom's nose again in a gesture of friendship.

Then, the magnificent, multi-legged caterpillar approached Tom and proclaimed, "My dear monster-in-training, may you grow another 38 legs, so you can establish your own private battalion of scouts."

Tom couldn't understand why anyone would think he needed a private battalion of scouts! His own two legs were quite sufficient for serving in any role, even a commander of a battalion. But Tom smiled politely.

The magnificent caterpillar lifted his upper body and clapped with his upper legs and feet to the rhythm of the music. Tom clapped in return, his sound pitifully weak in comparison to the amazing orchestration of the caterpillar.

Then the hunchback Cyclops, rolling his huge single eye, approached Tom. "My dear monster-in-training, may you grow a third eye in the center of your forehead, so that you can see the goings-on on the most distant stars, the way only trained Cyclops can do."

"What is it, exactly, that takes place on distant stars?" Tom asked with enthusiasm. He tried to picture himself with a third eye stuck in the middle of his forehead that could turn around like a telescope!

A deafening uproar broke out like waves as someone tried to push his way through the crowd.

"Quiet!" Hippo growled, "Ear-El the red cockroach also wants to offer his blessings."

Ear-El, all excited, jumped on his very own podium atop Rhino's horn, and declared, "I don't understand why I'm the one who is always interrupted."

"Carry on with your speech, please!" Hippo urged him.

Ear-El straightened his blue antennae, raised his head, and professed:

"The mighty elephant's trunk is very long,
And the rhino has just, a tough little horn.
The Cyclops has one big eye to stare,
And the caterpillar many legs to spare..."

"We know all that, we know all that," hissed the insects.

"We have heard this song before," chirped the ostrich.

"Let him finish!" Hippo growled again.

Ear-El continued:

"The giraffe's head rests on a lofty neck.
The ostrich's head is up or stuck in piles of sand.
But Tom's head is well planted in between his
shoulder blades."

While the monsters were wondering if they should boo or cheer, the elephants' band marched in and surrounded Tom on all sides, blowing their trumpets.

The tank wearing the coat of fresh flowers commanded: "One, two, and...three!"

And with their trunks, the elephants bounced Tom up and down...upward and downward, upward and downward, upward and downward.

Unprepared for such a swinging musical surprise and exhausted by all the excitement, Tom felt lightheaded and closed his eyes.

How much fun can you take?

CHAPTER 9

The Carnival Begins!

Tom opened his eyes.

I must be 200 years old by now.

The sound the elephants' band made blowing their trumpets in a joyful march brought a smile to his face.

Suddenly, the wings of the windmill began to rotate. Their color was no longer dusty grey but now vibrant red. Tiny red, yellow, and blue lights glimmered at the edges of the four wings, leaving behind sparkly trails, as the wings spun round and round. Tom watched in awe, noticing little hammocks attached to the rotating wings.

"Only small-sized monsters are allowed to ride the carousel!" announced prideful Hippo, always eager to serve in any significant capacity. Tonight, he was acting as the master of ceremonies.

Tom leapt high up on a wing and seated himself in one of the hammocks.

The crickets and other small insects soon followed, bouncing while holding on to the hammocks.

The chubby little pigs had a hard time hopping up. A graceful giraffe helped them up patiently, one piglet at a time.

As the speed of this merry-go-round increased, Tom's head spun. He felt like he was falling and falling, then the world was turning upside down. He marveled at the swirly motion.

Dizziness can sometimes be a very pleasant experience!

Three big bats drew near, flapping their wings in the clear night air and helping the windmill carousel spin faster. The tall giraffes were busy hanging colorful lanterns all over the kingdom. The first part of the carnival ended with thunderous drumming and lots of banging on cans. And then, the President of All Monsters, the mighty dinosaur, showed up, wearing an American Indian feather suit with two water pistols hanging from his belt. All the beasts stood in two long rows and cheered vigorously before making way for the president to pass through.

The kind-hearted dinosaur, known as an avid vegetarian, passed through the applauding monsters. His hind legs were long and bulky, while his front legs were short, thin, and well-manicured. His head, the size of an ostrich egg, rested proudly on his extended neck, a magnificent "hatter's hat" with peacock feathers crowning his scalp.

One owl flew closer to Tom, who by now

had gotten down from the merry-go-round, and whispered in his ear, "Mind you, the brainpower of the president is not much greater than the size of his head, but the beasts elected him because of his gigantic size. On the other hand," the owl went on explaining, "the king is truly blessed with great wisdom."

"And where is the king?" Tom asked.

The president stood on a stage that creaked under his enormous weight. He opened his mouth and cleared his throat at length before speaking.

The monsters, however, kept quiet in anticipation. Finally, he spoke.

"Tonight," said the president, "we will play the game Find the Dragon—our Dragon King. The dragon, as you all know by now, lives in a special palace known as the Temple of Puzzles and Puzzlement. There are many hallways and complicated passages in his palace. It is truly a maze.

"The dragon dwells in one of them. Whoever is the first to reach his majesty, the Dragon King, will be awarded the title of The Utmost Monstrous Monster in the Kingdom of Monsters. Finding the entrance to the palace is the personal responsibility of each and every beast that wishes to play the game. Although I am the president and the Dragon King's cousin, we all know that the dragon is our only true and wonderful ruler."

All of the monsters rose on their hind legs and cheered enthusiastically for quite some time.

Carefully, one foot at a time, President Dinosaur stepped down off the stage, and Gurgle the giraffe offered him a basket full of fresh carrots to satisfy his vegetarian tastes.

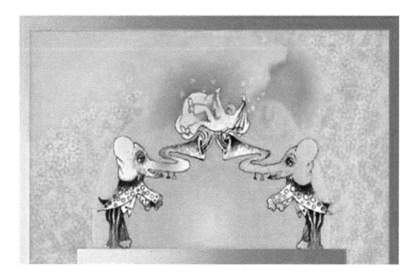

Fun Raising

CHAPTER 10

In the Temple of Puzzles
and Puzzlement

Tom was wandering around, inspecting the great piles of stuff near the windmill, when he noticed a sandbox.

Reaching down with cupped hands to collect some of the golden grains, Tom raised his arms with delight and let the sand drip slowly through his fingers.

Salty and soft sand from the seashore!

Looking down at the sandbox, he saw the sand spiraling around a growing hole in the ground. He tried to step into the opening.

This may be the entrance to the temple.

Suddenly, the opening grew wider, and Tom was sucked in, plunging into a dark and narrow tunnel.

Ahead, he could see four bright eyes blinking at short intervals, lighting the way. When he drew closer, Tom discovered a pair of owls standing motionless on a small reef. He thought they must be signaling something of great importance, but he could not figure out what.

Suddenly, it occurred to him that they could be operating as traffic lights in this tunnel. As he advanced, crawling under overhanging, curved rocks, the owls flew overhead and landed on

Tom's shoulders, illuminating the way for him like headlights.

This dark space horrifies me! I feel very out of place. I should turn back and get out of here!

But, when he turned around, the opening to the tunnel had disappeared. "If there is no way back, I have no other choice but to go forward and look for the king," he murmured to himself and shook the dust of the tunnel out of his curly, golden hair.

Miraculously, the tunnel expanded, and bright light streamed in from its far end. From that moment on, Tom could walk with greater ease, bending his back only slightly.

Facing the blinding light, his "headlights," the magnificent owls, blinked more rapidly. Apparently, they understood that their role had ended. Tom implored them to stay and keep him company, but they took off at once and vanished into the tunnel.

The walls of the tunnel now looked like a hallway, layered with smooth plaster textured with small, black-and-white checkerboard squares. Looking closer at the tiles' texture, he saw that the tiny white square tiles were painted with bright, glowing paint. Because the wall's surface was bumpy, the squares seemed uneven and confusing.

The hallway continued to expand, and soon the strangest, most monstrous beast came face to face with him. This monster was unlike any he had seen before—not among the Kingdom monsters nor in any of the zoology books he enjoyed reading. The strange creature had an elephant head and wore huge reading glasses. His torso resembled that of a horse though he had eagle wings, and his backside took the shape of a whale tail.

"And who are you?" asked the creature, removing his glasses.

"My name is Tom, and I am searching for the King of All Monsters," replied Tom politely. "Are you the Dragon-King?" he asked hopefully.

"I am the royal guardian of this place," answered the creature, closing the thick book he had been reading.

"Kids your age..." mumbled the mysterious creature, perhaps to himself, perhaps to Tom, "kids your age should be in bed already!"

That annoyed Tom.

"I don't get it! Why do you look so weird, and why do you need to make such a silly comment? And why... I am fed up explaining to everyone that I am Tom. Earlier this morning, I smashed the wicked alarm clocks that always interrupted my dreams, and now I am trying to find the King of All Monsters!"

"The King of All Monsters!" the creature imitated Tom's voice and burst out laughing. "What is the connection between broken clocks and the King of All Monsters? Calm down, sweet child, just cool it!"

Tom tried, but his thoughts churned.

If the temple guardian is so strange looking, I wonder how His Majesty the King looks?

The guardian seemed to have read his thoughts.

"If I were you, I would be quite content with the royal guardian, from whom you can learn so much more than from His Majesty himself. After all, kings are known to be very busy and preoccupied with kingly things."

"But I don't wish to learn anything in particular from the king. I simply need to find him!" Tom explained.

"And why is it so important for you to find the king?" asked the royal guardian, placing his reading glasses back on his nose.

"I don't know; I don't know," replied Tom in a puzzled tone, "I do not even understand how I got here. As soon as I entered the tunnel, I wanted to turn back, but I couldn't find the opening. And so, I kept going.

I dreamt once about meeting a king, any kind of king, and it didn't matter what kind of kingdom. And besides, a game is a game, and I do like playing a lot!"

"Aha!" said the creature, "very well, then. If you solve my puzzle, I will reveal to you how to proceed from here."

"I will give it a try."

"Who am I?"

"What?" Tom questioned.

"Who am I?" the creature repeated his question patiently, lifting his trunk to drive away a fly perched on one of his eagle wings.

"What?" Tom asked again. "How could I tell you who you are, if you don't know yourself?!"

The creature's glasses became covered with vapor; his majestic eagle wings folded inward, his whale tail tapped rhythmically on the floor, and his horse hoof nervously leafed through the book.

Not wanting to offend him, Tom said, "After all, everyone knows that you are the most honorable, scholarly, and illustrious royal guardian ever!"

The whale tail ceased tapping on the floor. A bright smile spread on the strange creature's face, as he said, "Pretty good, pretty good; you are getting closer. Would you like to try another guess?"

Tom thought a while longer. He lowered his gaze to the floor before raising his head and saying, "First of all, I must admit that never before have I met a magnificently glorious noble creature such as you."

"Really?" whispered the creature. His eagle wings opened up regally; his long trunk whirled in the air, and his eyes lit up in joy, hopping and leaping among the many books spread across the floor.

Tom smiled and continued, "Your head is like an elephant's head because the elephant is the wisest and the strongest of all animals. Your upper torso is horse-like because you like to gallop and go fast. You have eagle wings because you love flying and hope to land, one day, on top of the highest mountains. You have a whale tail because you like swimming in the ocean and hope to sail, one of these days, to the most distant seas, but, I wonder..." Tom's voice hesitated.

"What is it you wonder about?" the creature asked with curiosity.

"I wonder if you ever get away from this place. You look so very pale," said Tom.

For a split-second, the strange creature's face turned paler, but soon enough he recovered and said proudly, "And why should I leave this place, since I know everything about it?"

"If you know everything about this place, how is it that you don't know who you are?" Tom asked, laughing out loud, something he regretted instantly when he saw the royal guardian's tears.

"I am so sorry; I did not mean to hurt your feelings," Tom said softly, looking into the creature's eyes. "I bet that magnificent pair of reading glasses on your nose is a sign that you read many books and dream of reaching everywhere, everywhere at once. I think your name is Mr. Every-where!"

The strange, royal creature turned ruby red with excitement and began to dance, hopping and flipping in midair with amazing agility and grace, while singing aloud:

"My name is Every-where,
and anywhere I look I see myself
reflected everywhere!
And no creature could ever be so
happily busy as being me, anywhere, anywhere!
Every-where is my name,
but I am nowhere to be seen.
When I disappear somewhere,
it is just to reappear
Somewhere else in this amazing Maze..."

"Anyway, what was I about to say? Oh, yes, you are a smarty, boy!" mumbled Mr. Every-where, when he calmed down. "And now, it is my turn to help you. I will advise you on how to proceed on the path. I am not able to offer you a roadmap because the shape of this maze shifts from moment to moment. Listen carefully, then memorize my instructions:

Keep moving straight forward along the hallways. All the hallways are narrow, but when two animals wish to pass through at the same place and at the same time, the hallway suddenly expands and turns into a pleasant, inviting space, with wondrous music streaming in from somewhere. Do not linger anywhere too long, and never give in to any of the many enticing attractions that may come your way! It would make the road endless. When the straight path comes to an end, don't turn right or left. Be patient, wait, and think, and the road is sure to reopen and lead you where you need to go! "

Tom looked at the creature in awe.

"So long, then, and many blessings," said Mr. Every-where, mumbling softly to himself. His body shrank rapidly, and he disappeared into one of the shining squares on the wall.

Tom drew closer to the shining square, pounded on it with his fists, and cried, "Please, Mr. Every-where, stay for just a moment; I wish to ask one more question!" But to no avail; the wall became only that, an ordinary wall.

Who am I?

CHAPTER 11

The Hippo's Feast

Tom continued to walk through the hallway, though it was becoming smaller and smaller, until his head almost touched the ceiling.

Tom felt disheartened.

How very sad and boring to walk alone along this long and lonely hallway.

Just then, all of a sudden, the hallway widened, and Tom's old friend Hippo rolled over his head and stood just in front of him, smiling.

"Hello, Tommy," Hippo said in a cheery tone. "Would you care to join me for a light meal?"

"A meal?" Tom asked. "Is there a restaurant around here?"

"Soon you will find out," Hippo said, plucking an ornamented pin out of his hat and using it to clean his teeth of the remnants of his *last* meal.

Hippo hiccupped once, and a large inlaid tray hooked to chains appeared, slowly lowering from the ceiling. It was laden with all sorts of delicious foodstuffs, a feast for the eyes and the stomach: a big basket of fruits, tiny apples coated in honey, a pot of steaming hot chocolate, whipped cream pies with cherries on top, and other irresistible-looking delicacies.

Hippo hiccupped once again, and two large, checkered cubes sprang out of the ground. Hippo sat on one of the cubes and gestured to Tom to be seated on the other one.

"Excuse me, dear Hippo, but...I am in a rush," said Tom, just as the scent of the chocolate reached his nostrils, and his belly began to hum with hunger.

"Please be seated. There is no reason to hurry! It would be impolite to appear before the king famished."

Hippo's manner of speaking impressed Tom. He was the best mannered and gentlest of all the monsters. Tom had noticed that monsters who relish the pleasures of eating were kinder and less intimidating than the lean monsters.

"Thank you, Hippo. I'll just stand and have a quick bite," Tom said, helping himself to a cup of hot chocolate. He sipped the hot drink quickly and said, "Wonderful chocolate, absolutely delicious. It would complement perfectly a whipped cream pie with cinnamon flakes and a cherry on top."

"Please, help yourself to one," Hippo said, stretching out his hand and picking up, out of nowhere, a whipped cream pie with cinnamon flakes and a cherry on top, then offering it to Tom.

"Delightful pie, heavenly taste," he murmured, while licking his fingers, "but oddly enough, it tastes like a sweet banana."

"Then, by all means," said Hippo, and offered Tom a tray of bananas and exotic fruits.

"What a superb banana, truly superb! How strange that it tastes like soft, raw honey." Tom rejoiced in his delectable discoveries.

"That's it; that's it. Now you get it!" Hippo stomped his feet, pausing from eating momentarily, and repeated, "That's it; that's it! This is the utmost, sublime gastronomical pleasure there is: one kind of food tempts you for another kind. One taste leads to another, one smell evokes another, and the feast and pleasures of eating go on and on and on."

"So, no one ever finishes eating?" Tom cried out in alarm, now determined to leave at once before tempted to eat more and further delay his search for the king.

"What a fool! Will you ever learn the fine art of dining?" Hippo called after him, making his point by swallowing two peeled bananas, six whipped cream pies, and two apples coated in honey, all at once.

Tom ignored Hippo's entreaties and walked

on, whistling and singing, distancing himself from Hippo and his gastronomic temptations.

"The sun, from dawn to dusk, shines,
The stars, from dusk to dawn, twinkle
Love signs in the night sky
Hippo likes to chew and gobble,
So much so he starts to wobble.
Some kids nibble on one slice of bread
for a long while,
While others swiftly devour a whole loaf
and dare ask
For one slice more!"

"How does this song end?" Tom said to himself, trying hard to remember.

A voice came from overhead.

"More and more? Not anymore, not anymore. Less is more, less is more!"

It was Bluebeard, the witch, flying close by on her broom, a huge grasshopper following behind her.

"In other words, it's always best, kids, to eat your meals on time," hummed the grasshopper.

The odd pair slowed down momentarily, as Tom gazed up at them and remarked, "I wonder why I'm singing a kindergarten song! After all, I am eleven years old!"

"Memory is like an alarm clock," Bluebeard softly answered him, before speeding off again.

"Wait a moment!" Tom called out.

"Sorry, we are in a hurry," replied the grasshopper, rushing to catch up with Bluebeard.

"Now you get it!"

CHAPTER 12

The Case of Gurgle, the Talkative Giraffe

Tom returned to the hallway that, again, had become narrow and low.

This maze is quite confusing, but I'm beginning to somehow enjoy it.

Suddenly, the ceiling rose higher and higher, and the walls grew taller and taller. Looking up, Tom could hardly see the ceiling! Lowering his gaze, he saw Master Gurgle, the monster giraffe, marching toward him, mumbling to himself. Tom pricked up his ears, and this is what he heard:

"If Peter Piper picked a peck of pickled peppers, where's the peck of pickled peppers Peter Piper picked?"

"Why are you talking to yourself?" Tom spoke up.

"I am playing with words," replied Gurgle in a flat tone.

"What does that mean, playing with words?" Tom asked.

"It is hard to explain with words," replied Gurgle. He stared at the distant ceiling with the look of obscure expectation and continued muttering to himself:

"Glowing ceiling hanging low,
Hope is grim, and gloom is raw.

Floating ceiling looming high,
Heads are up, as faith may rise."

"Nice flow of words, Master Gurgle, but what do they mean?" Tom asked half jokingly, trying to communicate with the enormous, talkative giraffe.

Master Gurgle replied solemnly, "Well, I will try to explain. I am used to thinking aloud because this is the only way I know. When I am silent, I actually stop thinking, so I must keep talking to keep thinking. And when there is no one around to talk to, I go on practicing, playing with words and twisting my tongue in the process. Is that clear?" Gurgle raised his head proudly. "I must confess it is not often that I have the chance to impart such a complicated explanation to such an attentive listener, curious about my creative process."

"Very strange," Tom mused, "Our teacher taught us that we think in silence; we should talk only after we have finished thinking, and playing with words is just a goofy game!"

"Nonsense," said Gurgle and burst out laughing. "I ran away from school when I was in first grade. I don't like being told what to do, how to figure things out, or when to speak. After all, the school system in Giraffe-land does not suit a talkative giraffe like me!"

Joyous and giddy with his talking and thinking, he rotated his head on its long neck.

"What did you do after running away from school?" Tom inquired.

"While my friends suffered through school, I began making a living, working at the national Giraffe-land amusement park. I had my own, very popular, daily talk show and made lots of new friends. I had many pals to play with and lots of opportunities to talk, talk, talk, and talk some more."

"But don't we have to listen, too, to hear what is being said? You can't go on talking nonstop." Tom tried to get a word in, but Master Gurgle, yawned as if disinterested, and continued talking.

"To listen, to be all ears? So very few can. Most pretend to be listening; this is why no one hears. To be honest with you, I have no time or patience to practice this 'listening and hearing' thing. As I have told you, I simply love to talk!"

"So perhaps you know, and can tell me, where is the king?"

Gurgle looked in the other direction and, oddly, kept quiet.

"Are you playing the game 'Find the Dragon?'" Tom asked.

Gurgle made an unclear gesture with his ears. Tom could not tell if Gurgle's gesture meant yes or no. Then, clearly angered, Gurgle demanded,

"Why are you asking so many questions? Have you mistaken me for a talking electric pole, or a talking traffic sign with arrows and flashing lights? I am only a fun-loving giraffe, who likes to take long walks and talk a lot!"

Annoyed, Tom looked Gurgle up and down.

I think Gurgle would have done better to stay in school, at least until the eighth grade. Perhaps, then, he would have learned to listen.

Gurgle seemed to have calmed down a bit. As if he did not want to miss a chance to chatter, he answered Tom's question. "The king? The king? Of course, I'm looking for the king! After all, who isn't searching for the king? Everyone I know, except for the king himself, is yearning to find the king. The king owns treasures; the king rules the kingdom; the king has a queen; the king has advisers, dancers, monkeys, servants, and guardians...the king has got it all!"

Tom's face flushed with irritation, and he burst out, "Get to the point! Get to the point! You never get to the point!"

"Why are you so upset?" Gurgle muttered and gazed again at the high ceiling. "Look, look up! You can hardly see the end of it."

"The end of what?" Tom inquired, looking up.

"You cannot see the ceiling, of course!" Gurgle exclaimed, pointing up, "And the king is way up there, where else?"

"Up there? How can we get up there from here?"

"In this maze of self-discovery, wonderful things may happen," replied Gurgle. "Soon this lofty ceiling will drop down and we will ascend up there, quickly... but not yet."

"Really?" Tom said, as if trying to remember something. "Do you know why memory is like an alarm clock?"

Gurgle smiled sweetly and said, "Yes, of course, memory is like a bell ringing gently in my mind, awakening a tale I once heard or a tail of a tale I need to grab onto." Gurgle added: "At times, it is like the chiming of bells, ringing chapters into a long tale I have lived to tell. Did you hear what I just heard?"

"No, what was it?"

"A bell ringing, reminding me of yet another tale I wish to tell before the ceiling descends," continued Gurgle. "It is a story about my cousin, a charming lady giraffe named Poetic-ah, whose fame has spread throughout all of Giraffe-land..."

"If I have to wait, I might as well listen," Tom thought to himself.

Gurgle went on talking excitedly, his long neck stretching up and down as he spoke.

"Poetic-ah, the lady giraffe I mentioned, was a champion of storytelling. She once worked as a teacher in the municipal kindergarten of Giraffe-land. Every morning, she would gather up all the baby giraffes and tell them wonderful stories, full of suspense. When Poetic-ah finished telling a story, her thin and delicate neck would grow an inch or two longer. The baby giraffes and their neighbors would point in admiration and envy at Poetic-ah's neck. Before long, her neck became known as the longest and most graceful in all of Giraffe-land.

"Still, she did not let the praise distract her from her dedication to her profession. To the contrary, the taller her neck grew, the more fascinating and suspenseful her stories became. Until one bright day, when she was in the midst of storytelling, all excited, a toddler giraffe stood up and asked,

'Poetic-ah, I didn't understand you. What was the word you just said, was it a wizard or a lizard?'

"All at once, more toddlers lifted their necks

and inquired: 'And the word before that, was it a cake on a plate or a skate on a gate?'

'And yesterday, in the story about the boat, did you say a boat or a goat?'

"Poetic-ah answered each and every question patiently. She decided that from now on she should raise her voice, but this did not help. Her neck continued to grow longer and longer, but her voice could barely be heard.

"One day, when she was frustrated with all the questioning and inquiring, she rose to her full height. Straining her voice, she exclaimed as loudly as she could:

'A lizard is not a wizard, nor is it a blizzard.
A cake on a plate cannot skate on a gate.
And goats cannot sail at sea like boats.'

"The next day, not a single baby giraffe showed up at the kindergarten. Poetic-ah withdrew, sour-faced and disappointed.

"On weekends, the grownups would take their little ones for a walk to the place where Poetic-ah had retreated, walking in circles around her favorite acacia tree. They would greet her with great respect and whisper to the little ones, 'This is Poetic-ah, whose neck grew longer and longer. Once she was known for her beautiful and spirit-lifting stories. But nowadays, no toddler giraffe

can hear her, let alone understand what she is
talking about. Watch out, little ones, don't grow
up too fast, remember Poetic-ah!'

"Poetic-ah's grief did not last long. One
morning, her head popped up above the treetops.
She looked up and down and began telling stories
to the birds.

"And thus," concluded Gurgle, "a wonderful
solution was found. A new, short-necked
kindergarten teacher was assigned to teach the
toddler giraffes, while the birds congregated around
the overjoyed Poetic-ah to listen to her stories."

"Truly, a remarkable story," Tom agreed, "but when is the ceiling going to come down? And when are we going to see the king?" Tom began to doubt what Gurgle had said earlier about the descending ceiling. But, since he had no idea where to go next, he decided to wait for a while longer.

Gurgle wiped the perspiration from his forehead, sighed, folded his hind legs to lower his body, and continued to mumble to himself quietly.

"Well, then…" continued Gurgle, his voice strengthening, as he lifted himself up on his four legs. "One day, Poetic-ah fell in love with a red boar. Her entire family was opposed to the match. After all, who has ever heard of a gifted, gentle lady giraffe falling for a wild, red boar? But Poetic-ah insisted, 'I do love my Tore, and he is my one and only wondrous, fabulous, and brave red boar!'

"Truth be told," Gurgle lowered his voice, "Tore was hard-of-hearing, but he loved looking at Poetic-ah, adoring her tall, pretty figure. Whenever she opened her mouth to recite one of her many tales, his face would light up like the full moon, and he would nod at length in appreciation and approval.

"Poetic-ah's father was very strict, and he made up his mind to put an end to the strange affair. He locked her in a large cage made of very sturdy and tall bamboo, but Tore would not give up. Each night, he would stand in front of the bamboo cage, stretching up his short neck and howling into the darkness like a coyote in the desert—so enamored of Poetic-ah was he. The other boars made fun of his heart-wrenching howls. This hurt Tore deeply. One night, he returned to his beloved and in a fit of anger broke through the cage with his sharp teeth, freeing Poetic-ah. Together, they fled to Africa and settled on a plantation thick with bananas.

"For many years, Poetic-ah's family grieved. Her strict father would send secret messages to her via an adventurous dove, which fancied a winter vacation in Africa.

"After a long while, seized by deep longing for her family, Poetic-ah returned from Africa. Tore, who had become quite heavy and lost his agility and gracefulness, accompanied her, along with their many children."

"Children!" Tom said, "I wonder what their children looked like?"

"Ah!" Gurgle giggled, as he rolled his eyes. "Well, some of their offspring resembled wild boars, but were boastful like lofty giraffes, while the rest looked like lofty giraffes, but, shameful to admit, they behaved like pigs."

"That reminds me of some children I know," Tom giggled.

"Yes, indeed," Gurgle agreed. "But, never pass judgment on others based on appearance only."

"True, so true," Tom said, nodding his head. "You must experience how others behave. It's good to have a conversation, be together for a while, before forming an opinion."

"Chatting? Conversing?" Gurgle could hardly hold back a burst of laughter. "What I like doing is talking, just talking! Don't you get it?"

"Maybe, but I must think about it some more," Tom replied, as he was about to teach Gurgle a little lesson. But before he could proceed, the ceiling came down and swung about three feet above Gurgle's head.

The ceiling now revealed a small opening and, at that very moment, out of nowhere, the friendly rhino showed up.

"How lovely, one of my favorite fans, the fabulous rhino, here to see me," rejoiced Gurgle. "Did you hear the funny story about the ostrich?"

"Gurgle, Gurgle, it's time to stop, Gurgle," Tom called out and pulled at Gurgle's tail. "There is no more time for tales! We must go up right now! It was you who told me about this opening in the ceiling. And now, after such a long wait, here it is!"

"All right, all right," Gurgle said casually, "you go first!"

"I can't, it is too high."

Gurgle grabbed Tom by his pants and lifted him straight up to the ceiling.

Tom jumped into the opening, looked down, and called out, "Now it's your turn!"

"Patience, patience, I can't stop in the middle of a sentence," Gurgle said, and turned to Rhino. At that very moment, the opening closed up.

Tom gazed in disbelief at the closed opening and said to himself, "I have never met such a talkative creature in my whole life. Everything reminds him of something else until he forgets where he came from and where he is heading. And now his endless talking has prevented him from following me into the ceiling."

Poetic-ah in love

CHAPTER 13

Tom's Battle with the Flies

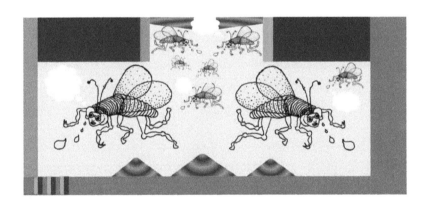

Tom turned from the sealed opening and looked around. He found himself in a new hallway with walls so high he could hardly see the ceiling.

"This hallway's similar to the other one, without the talkative giraffe," Tom mused aloud. "Actually, it would not be a bad idea to bring Gurgle to my schoolyard one day, so he could entertain the kids with his fantastical tales."

"Indeed, why not bring the giraffe to your school?" asked a funny-looking bat that suddenly flew over Tom's head.

"A giraffe would not get along with any of my teachers," Tom replied, but the bat was already gone.

The corridor gradually expanded, and the checkerboard squares on the walls were turning round and round. Soft armchairs were scattered about. The floor, though flat, looked wavy because of the way it was painted, making Tom dizzy as if he was seasick. Worn out from the long walk, Tom collapsed into one of the armchairs. He had closed his eyes and begun to doze off when a sudden, deafening buzz startled him awake.

Opening his eyes, he saw a huge fly, as

big as a sheep, hovering around his head. Tom waved his arms, trying to drive it away. The fly took flight but soon returned and resumed his annoying buzzing.

"Go away!" Tom hollered and jumped to his feet.

"It is impolite to use such harsh words, especially when talking to your host! After all, you are in the House of Flies," buzzed the fly, sounding offended.

"So sorry," said Tom, "I had no idea that this is the House of Flies."

"In fact," the fly continued calmly, "very few creatures in the Maze of Puzzles and Puzzlement know this as the House of Flies, but," his voice suddenly loud and clear, "my famous grandfather, the grand sage Achitophel, claims it to be so. And when my grandfather, who named me Oz, acknowledges something to be so, then so be it." Oz the fly concluded his speech with a noisy buzz.

Tom was tired and didn't wish to get into an argument with a bothersome fly, so he chose to speak softly and evenly.

"Perhaps this is the House of Flies, perhaps not. Perhaps it is just one more long, nameless corridor. I don't know, and I don't care to know. All I need right now is to get some rest. And when I am resting, I appreciate peace and quiet."

"How dare you doubt what I say?" Oz cried out, irritated, and clearly off the subject. "My grandfather, Achitophel, says that flies, too, deserve a comfortable, respectable-looking house. And, moreover, my grandfather insists that the time has come to change the course of history!"

"What do you mean by change the course of history?" Tom asked in a tired, irritated voice.

"It means that instead of starving flies chasing humans and spoiling their meals, it's about time that humans deliver food to the House of Flies! Is that understood? Well, then, if you want to take a rest, be my guest. But remember, you are only a guest in the House of Flies!" Red with excitement, the fly concluded his speech.

Tom didn't care much about the importance of the place where he happened to rest, and he didn't understand why this buzzing fly seemed so eager to argue with him. So, he simply closed his eyes, ignoring the fly, and sank deeply into the soft armchair.

Soon, a loud buzzing sound interrupted his peace once again.

Tom opened his eyes and yawned, the same giant fly before him, "How can I possibly get some rest with all this noise around me, mainly due to you!"

"I am tired, too," grumbled Oz and gathered up his noisy wings.

"Why don't you take a break and rest, too? There are plenty of armchairs around," Tom responded more politely.

"I am hungry, and I can't rest before I am well fed," Oz whined. "And, besides, as I said before, here in the House of Flies the guests feed the hosts. Otherwise, why have a House of Flies in the first place?"

Tom thought he had the solution and pulled a big banana out of his pocket that he had saved from Hippo's feast. He peeled it carefully, then graciously served it to the flying giant.

"I don't like bananas!"

"Spoiled monster fly!" Tom said, "Taste this banana, and you will know the true taste of fresh honeydew."

"A banana is just a banana," protested Oz. "Honeydew I like, but bananas I detest."

"Although large in size, a fly is still a fly!" Tom grinned and bit the top off of his banana.

But, this fly was truly hungry. He zoomed in, buzzing around Tom's head, and, sure enough, grabbed the banana and devoured all that remained in just one bite.

"You were right! This banana tastes like

honey. Really good! Perhaps you have another one?" the fly begged, for something he had detested just moments before.

"This was a very special one," Tom said with enthusiasm, "a takeout souvenir from my feast with Hippo, where everything you taste reminds you of another sublime delicacy, so you keep on eating and..."

"...you never finish eating," the fly completed Tom's sentence.

"How did you know?" Tom asked.

"Ah! The hippo's feast, the hippo's feast... Who doesn't dream of being invited one day to the hippo's feast?" the fly sighed deeply, his voice trembling with excitement.

"My grandfather, the grand sage Achitophel, was privileged to be one of the very few in the entire world to have been summoned to the hippo's feast," the fly continued, begging still for another banana.

"I am so sorry," Tom said while turning out his empty pockets. "There are no more bananas!"

The fly continued to hover and circle around Tom, landing on and off on his head.

"Stubborn fly, I swear to you, I have no more bananas. Please let me rest; I am so very tired!"

"Remember, according to the custom in the

House of Flies," the fly buzzed, stressing every word, "our guests must feed us, their hosts, and only then do we allow them to move about freely."

"When in the House of Flies…" Tom mumbled. He recalled a similar saying that he had once learned in history class. Wishing to appease the fly, Tom took a white handkerchief out of his pocket and a pair of gloves. "Perhaps you would like a taste," he said hopefully.

"Shame on you, naughty you!" the offended fly spat, swinging his huge wings and buzzing on. "Are you mistaking me for a washing machine?"

"I'm sorry!" Tom responded with a conciliatory tone, "but I truly don't have any more bananas."

"If you can't meet our standards, you better get out of here, now!" the fly said sharply.

"Who says this place is really the House of Flies?" Tom asked, trying to rescue himself from what was now a stressful situation.

"That's enough, certainly enough!" the fly now raged, attaching his mouth to a huge funnel and crying out, "Listen up to what this cheeky boy has to say!"

From all sides, flocks of big flies accompanied by herds of smaller flies flew in and circled around the terrified Tom, buzzing and punching him with their wings.

Suddenly, Tom knew what to do! He spread his magnificent bat wings, and by weaving his way quickly through the crowd of circling flies, he managed to escape unharmed.

Strange that using my wings had not occurred to me. They can save me from real danger or even unexpected war.

Tom basked in the freedom of his flight, slowing only to smooth and straighten the wrinkles in his bat outfit, admiring its material.

I am eleven years old, and, already, I have participated in two wars. I fought the clocks and then the giant flies, and I survived. I had never intended to fight anyone or anything. Perhaps all creatures, large or small, will fight, rightly or wrongly, for what they believe are their rights! Even flies fight for their rights! And who would have ever believed that?

Tom now flew along the long hallway when he noticed Bluebeard flying toward him. "Hey, Tom, your appearance alarmed me! What's up?" The witch commented, as she slowed down.

"Those flies almost drove me out of my mind!" Tom sighed. "One named Oz fought me over a banana shortly after I'd offered him my last one, the one I kept in my pocket from the hippo's feast!"

"Yes, they don't make much sense, not to

mention how arrogant and pretentious they are," Bluebeard whispered.

"Yes, especially their leader, the one who claims to be the grandson of Achitophel!" Tom sighed, suddenly noticing a dark buzzing cloud of flies approaching from the other end of the hallway.

"Are they still after me?" Tom raised his voice, turning to Bluebeard, "Hold on, watch out!"

Bluebeard kept her composure. Facing the approaching flies, she called out, "Peace be with you!" and pointed the end of her broom toward the buzzing gang.

"Peace is good, but a piece of cake is even better," exclaimed the flying giant leading the gang. It was Oz!

"Peace is the real way, but peace is not always a piece of cake! You have to work at it and pave the way, piece by piece," Bluebeard advised.

"How come?" Oz asked, buzzing impatiently.

"By walking on walls, holding still to ceilings, gluing your feet to the bare reality, letting go of anger while contemplating the wonders of an upside-down world," explained Bluebeard.

"Sounds compelling," remarked the winged creature after some pondering and gazing at the walls. "I will ponder it and consider putting a new twist on my act the next time I walk my talk on walls or hang from ceilings." Brushing his front legs together against his chest as if begging, he winked at Tom, "Please forgive us, but we are still very hungry, and a simple piece of bread will also do."

"Sorry, I don't have a piece of bread, but I can offer a piece of advice. It's all right to ask, but it's wrong to make demands. Because you asked me nicely, I will let you in on the big news about Mr. Hippo. He has decided to go on a diet, so he can share more doggy bags with those less fortunate."

"Thank you, off we go," buzzed Oz.

"I must depart too," announced Bluebeard and flew off in the opposite direction.

"Wait a minute," Tom tried to stop them.

All of a sudden, he found himself travelling solo again, free of company, but thankfully also free of the fly problem.

"In the house of flies, behave like a fly."

CHAPTER 14

The Weigh-Master Cockroach

A faint voice echoed along the walls. "Yes, yes, yes, every creature in the whole wide world is entitled to fight injustice."

Tom slowed his flapping wings, flying slowly, up and down, back and forth, searching along the tall walls. He saw many hollow cubicles, but he could not tell where the faint voice came from.

"Greetings, my friend Tom, I'm right here in the corner."

Tom looked around again and discovered the red cockroach Ear-El, sitting in a dim corner next to a large pair of scales. He had landed on a hollow cube sticking out of the wall and folded his wings.

"Greetings to you, too, my friend," said Tom. "How could you hear my thoughts?"

"I have a pair of antennae!" Ear-El smiled, shaking his blue antennae joyfully.

"Do your antennae work like radar?" Tom asked curiously.

"More or less," Ear-El smiled mysteriously and muttered, "anyway, every creature in the whole wide world, particularly here, in the Maze of Puzzles and Puzzlement, is entitled to fight for justice!"

"In matters of justice, you are absolutely right," Tom replied, "but if you could only see how those flies behaved!"

"Justice is justice! And a fly is a fly! And unless flies protest and put out flyers to express their plight, right may turn into wrong and wrong may turn into right! I can't say anything because I'm not familiar enough with this case, yet."

"Then go and see for yourself," Tom suggested. "The flies could use a lesson or two from you!"

Ear-El bent his antennae, shook his head, and said in a sad voice, "After all, most of the monsters, and especially the flies, harass me shamelessly! They keep saying that everyone strives for justice; it is the just thing to do when wronged! Yet, no one is willing to hear what a scholar like me has to say about justice!" He sighed and looked at Tom. "You were there, so perhaps you recall what it took for the hippo to calm down the monsters when I asked for permission to speak before the game was to begin," Ear-El quivered, as he straightened his trembling antennae.

Tom regarded Ear-El.

What a poor, miserable cockroach.

"Do not pity me!" Ear-El thundered. "Mercy may interfere with the measure of justice, in general, and with me, in particular."

"I was just thinking, just thinking to myself..." Tom tried to calm the offended cockroach.

"Don't forget that I have antennae that can read thoughts," Ear-El smiled.

"What do you intend to do in the meantime?" Tom asked.

"Oh, in the meantime?" Ear-El stopped playing with the scales.

"I mean, until justice shows itself! Until the monsters learn to listen with respect."

Ear-El looked up and whispered, "In the meantime, I weigh things."

"Weigh things? What do you weigh?" Tom asked with curiosity.

"I weigh and check how many flies match the weight of one flounder. I weigh and check how many flounders match the weight of one hippopotamus. I weigh and check how many hippos match the weight of one dinosaur."

"Yes, yes, I got it already," Tom interrupted the flow of Ear-El's speech and said, "It reminds me of a lesson in algebra, when the teacher asks, 'How many times does the number two go into ten?' Why do you weigh things in the first place?" Tom asked.

"What else is there to do?" Ear-El said in a quiet and restrained voice.

"How about doing nothing, for a change?" suggested Tom.

Ear-El looked alarmed when he replied, "Nothing? How do you do that?"

"How? You do the undo! Odds are up for you, as you undo the knots and bolts of bullying," a familiar voice sounded, as Bluebeard landed on a nearby cube. "Greetings and blessings to my old warrior pal Ear-El," said Bluebeard, "and don't worry, you can do the undo!"

Bluebeard turned to Tom, "And you can, too!"

"How can I do the undo?" Ear-El uttered after a long pause.

"Listen to your purpose," Bluebeard said.

"What is my purpose?" asked Ear-El.

"To listen," said Bluebeard, putting her right hand over her heart.

"I listen all the time, and my ears only hurt," Ear-El mumbled.

Tom nodded in agreement.

Bluebeard took her stand again and proclaimed,

"Time to listen in a new way:
Listen to your breath,
Listen to the winds,
Listen deep, so you may hear.
The little voice within you sings.
Time to weigh ideas, not only things,
Time to draw new measures, time to Imagine
An empty shell and oneself as a brand-new shelf."

Beaming with sudden joy, Ear-El declared, "I love it! Thank you, I feel so much taller now." Ear-El smiled happily and went on rocking the scales up and down, up and down, mumbling to himself:

"A habit is a habit, what can you do?
A habit is a habit you can undo."

"Before I leave, I have a question for you," Tom said.

Ear-El's face brightened up again as his thin antennae danced in midair. "At last, someone is consulting me!"

"Perhaps you can tell me where I can find the king?"

"Ah!" Ear-El said solemnly and folded his antennae. "You ask 'where is the king?' but I don't think you have asked the right question."

"What should I ask?" Tom stuttered.

"According to my reasoning, you should be asking, 'Who is the king?' And only after posing such a question may you proceed to the next one: 'Where is the king?'"

Roles and Rules

"But if I knew in advance who the king was, there would be no surprise, and a game without surprises is not a game. Have you forgotten already that this is just a game?"

"You have forgotten that I, too, participate in the game 'Find the Dragon,'" said Ear-El.

"So, let us play the game together; after all, we are already old friends," suggested Tom.

"No, thanks," said Ear-El, "I am playing this game by *my* rules. First, I need to figure out who could possibly be the king. Only then will I be on my way."

"If you insist on playing this game by your rules, how can we be partners?" asked Tom, flapping his wings, as he and Bluebeard took off in different directions.

"Peace and good luck!" Ear-El called out.

Tom hovered high up the hallway, thinking, "It is not every day that one encounters friendly beings to chat with."

CHAPTER 15

Jack the Shark Teaches Tom a Lesson in Friendship

Tom was enjoying every moment of flying through the long corridors. He remembered the aircraft he once saw performing amazing aerobatics. Tom soared higher, turned upside down in a sharp angle, diving, and soaring up again. Over and over he dove and soared until he landed on one of the cubes that bulged from the wall.

I could go on flying forever, but the flies' nuisance has passed, and it is time to come down.

He walked forward, his hands stretched out to the sides, swaying from side to side.

It is a strange feeling to be walking again after such a long, delightful flight. Only now can I understand why birds never linger in one place.

Tom gazed longingly at the high ceiling.

Gradually, the corridors expanded, opening into a large, wide hall.

Master Every-where gave me some very useful advice, but he did not tell me what to do if I reached a space with walls all alike, with no windows or doors.

Tom stood perplexed at the center of this empty space as wide as a ballroom. Suddenly, a square door opened in the wall. Festive music sounded, and a small band of white mice marched in. Tom ran toward the square door, but it closed before he could reach it. At the other end of the hall, another square door opened up, and a procession of piglets dressed like clowns marched through it, holding colorful torches in their hands.

Again, Tom ran toward the open door, but it, too, closed as rapidly as it had opened.

"First, I need to look carefully around," Tom said aloud, observing the many squares embedded in the walls. He noticed that one wall was more yellowish than the other walls.

I will stand by this wall until something happens.

Long moments passed with nothing happening. Tom was getting bored.

Out of boredom, he began knocking on the plaid pattern of the yellow wall, hoping to find an opening. "This wall is different from the rest of the walls; therefore, the gateway out might be here," he again mused aloud.

While he continued tapping on the wall and pondering, a square window opened in the floor and a strong wind blew up from the opening. Impulsively, Tom jumped into the new opening, landing softly on the floor. He gathered himself and looked around. "This must be the basement of the hall. It's different from the floor above," Tom exclaimed.

Suddenly

Instead of a checked pattern on the walls, wavy lines adorned these walls, creating the impression of perpetual motion. Even the floor seemed to constantly move forward, undulating in a rising and falling movement.

Tom climbed up the steep slope and slid down the slippery slant. Again and again, up and down, up and down, he went. His wooden shoes widened and grew larger and larger until he stood like Gulliver in the land of the Lilliputians, feet planted in two boats.

The boat-like shoes moved on their own wavy path: rising, sliding, and slipping; rising, sliding, and slipping. Tom was thrilled. "Some wonderful surprises have happened to me today," he said to himself. "First, I flew up high. Then, I sailed in a pair of shoe-boats. And now, this path of wonder pulls me along with such ease and grace. I feel blessed."

He was laughing happily, not quite noticing the tremendous distance he had travelled. Suddenly, he had to stop short, faced with a shark as tall as a two-story building.

"Ohhh, no, ohh boy, this is some scary checkpoint," Tom said, shivering.

The shark smiled and blocked the passage with its mighty body.

Tom kept his composure and said, "Hello, Mr. Shark. Would you kindly make room for me to pass through? I am in a hurry to reach the King of All Monsters!"

"No, you can't pass through," replied the shark flatly and smiled again.

"Why not?" Tom trembled, another shiver traveling down his spine.

"I am looking for a friend," the shark said,

with a serious expression. "My name is Jack," he
added casually.

A friend?

Tom couldn't imagine who that could be,
looking up at the enormous creature.

*To be a friend of a creature whose height is
nearly thirty feet, is it truly possible?*

Tom pondered his own question, raising his
eyes to look into the eyes of the shark.

*If I had a friend—a golden fish in a jar,
I would no doubt be the happiest kid on
Earth! I would feed him three times a day
and refresh the water in the jar every single
day, too. I could be happy just looking at the
colors of his glowing scales and his elegant*

swimming motion in that little wet universe of his. But what can I do for a shark? What can a shark do for me? And what can we do together as friends?

"You don't have to do anything for me," the shark said, as if he had read Tom's thoughts. "You just have to believe I'm your friend. Then, I

will swallow you whole. Just hop into my jaws," Jack said in a cheerful voice.

"Swallow me?" Alarmed, Tom searched for a fast way out.

But Jack, the mighty shark, blocked the

tunnel completely. "Yes, swallow you. And this will be the beginning of a wonderful friendship!" Jack laughed heartily, and the sound of his merriment rolled down the hall and back, echoing as a wave bouncing back to shore.

"What a strange friendship; if you swallow me, I will be no more," Tom said, quite unnerved.

"Don't be afraid, boy. My name is Jack, and yours is Tom. Sharks with a kid's name never hurt kids. I will swallow you here and throw you up there, well and sound. Trust me!"

"Why? Why do you have to swallow me? Can't you simply guide me on my way to find the King of All Monsters?"

"No," said the shark in a very strict voice with a brief smile. "This is my style of friendship, and I do it my way. I swallow my friends and deliver them safely to where they wish to be going."

"Traveling within you. Wow! I wonder what's it like," Tom pondered and gazed into Jack's big, blue eyes. "Is a shark like an underwater bus, a fish-like submarine, or...?"

Suddenly, the shark opened his jaws, and Tom found himself seated on the soft, pink tongue inside Jack's mouth. "It has been quite a while since I took a bath," Tom said to himself. As soon as he said it, clear and comfortably warm jets of water washed him from head to toe. He played in the water that filled the concave tongue of his newfound friend, Jack.

I wish I could have undressed before bathing. It would be difficult to dry up now.

He got up and out of the tongue-bathtub.

A pleasant breeze began to blow over him and into a dark, round opening at the root of Jack's tongue. The wind caressed Tom and pulled him into the hole, the shark's throat. He rolled and fell down Jack's throat, while his clothes dried in the warm, pleasant wind that drew him downward.

"What a wonderful place," Tom marveled aloud upon arriving in the shark's belly.

Jack is not an ordinary shark. His inside is like a palace within a submarine, more amazing than any of the royal courts I have read about in history books. And I am the first kid ever to visit such a splendid place!

The shark's round ribs seemed like beautiful arched pillars rising on either side of the palatial space. Pretty armchairs made of conches and padded with sea sponges were spread all around. Tom dropped into one of the inviting chairs. After such fun bathing, his stomach rumbled for a hearty meal.

Out of nowhere, a friendly octopus appeared,

wearing a large chef's hat. Food trays made of shiny shells rested on each of his eight arms. Two tall eels wearing black bowties followed him. They placed a small coral bush next to Tom. It held a large pearly tray. The octopus arranged the food on the pearly tray and quipped, "Enjoy your meal!" The delicious, aromatic smell of hot seafood reached Tom's nose.

"It is truly a royal meal, so enticing," Tom said aloud. He had no idea what to try first.

Two ladyfish approached from the far end of the hall, tiptoeing on their tails. They were wrapped in elegant, embroidered robes and long tulle trains with delicate, lacy patterns.

Tom recalled a similar lace robe he once saw in a picture depicting a French queen from a

bygone era. The beautiful ladyfish came closer.

These are not really lace gowns. These are fish scales, breathing gills and fins, more beautiful than any embroidery in the whole wide world.

At that moment, the two ladyfish embarked on an enchanting and most captivating dance.

I wish they would sing while dancing.

As if they could read Tom's thoughts, the ladyfish and the eels shook their heads.

I wonder what they mean. Perhaps they want silence, an important feature of true friendship.

He remembered Gurgle, the talkative giraffe, and chuckled to himself.

Tom relished his meal in the peaceful splendor of Jack's belly. When he had finished, his friendly hosts cleared the trays. Soon after, a gentle movement rocked the place.

It's like swinging in a hammock.

Tom giggled with delight, before noticing a large, bright passage at the end of the hall. A strong wind blew, carrying Tom out of the shark's belly.

"Everything's going so fast!" Tom exclaimed, as he stood up.

Directly in front of him, stood Jack, the mighty shark.

Jack turned his tail to the left and instructed kindly, "From here on, Tom, go straight forward. Good luck to you, and many thanks."

"You are grateful to *me*? I am the one who feels grateful for everything, first and foremost your amazing hospitality," Tom shared.

"It's okay, Tom, that's just my style of friendship," Jack said, "I appreciate my friendly guests." Jack smiled, revealing two rows of huge, white teeth.

"Thank you, thank you, Jack, and goodbye!" Tom called after him, as Jack's tail disappeared in the distance.

Tom was happy to have found a kind and helpful friend like Jack in this tumultuous kingdom, even though he found it strange that his new friend was a shark and a mighty one at that!

One never knows where and how true friendship may arise!

Tom smiled widely, as he walked onto the paved road that stretched before him.

CHAPTER 16

The Seventh Meeting

There were no more checkered or wavy corridors, only straight, thin lines etched along the walls. Tom looked at the floor and realized he was walking barefoot. "I must have lost my shoes in the shark's belly," he said to himself sadly.

But it's not a great loss, really. The shoes were large and clumsy, and here I am walking on a new path that is soft and comfortable like the sand on the beach.

Tom looked ahead and saw a green, wooden bridge. Across the bridge lay a spacious, island-like square laden with flowers. He crossed the bridge and stood at the gate to the island of flowers.

A wide variety of flowers were in glorious bloom on this island—violets, primroses, roses, and daisies, as well as less common flowers, such as orchids, birds-of-paradise, nasturtiums, tropical and subtropical flowers, and other splendid blooms whose names he didn't know. Tom found it odd that the flowers were all closed and slightly bent.

"Maybe this is the municipal park of the Kingdom of Monsters, and they are resting someplace else," Tom reasoned as he looked around the island.

Looking closely toward the center of the island of flowers, he saw a most beautiful sight that caught his breath. In one of the flowerbeds, a lovely, tall flower-maiden, as tall as Tom herself, rested peacefully, her eyes closed.

The flowerbed lay at the foot of an apple tree laden with ripe fruit. At the end of one branch, a spider-monster was busy weaving a fine golden mesh that dropped down gently and covered the sleeping beauty.

"What a pretty golden mesh," Tom shared with the spider-monster.

"It is meant to protect her," replied the spider-monster and pointed to the sleeping flower-maiden.

"Protect her from what?" Tom inquired.

"From flies and other pests," said the spider-monster as he threaded another golden strand through the eye of the needle he was using to weave the golden mantle.

"And when will she wake up?"

"When the darkness ends, and the air is warmer," replied the spider-monster.

"Who is she waiting for?" asked Tom, gazing again at the sleeping beauty.

"Perhaps you," the spider-monster replied cryptically.

"Me? How could she possibly know that I might be arriving?"

"She has no clue, but she has been waiting."

Tom gently lifted the golden web and looked in amazement at the pretty flower-maiden, who was turning from side to side.

All the flowers in the garden began to move in unison, to and fro, like the waves of the sea. The flower-maiden rubbed her eyes and began to spin around. A mane of blossoms rippled around her, spiraling up in the morning wind.

"Touch her, touch her now," whispered the spider-monster. Tom touched her hand, and the flower-maiden opened her eyes wide. At that very moment, all the flowers stood upright and spread their magnificent petals.

"Soon the dawn will rise," whispered the flower-maiden.

"Soon the dawn will rise," whispered the other flowers.

"The pink, rosy dawn ānd the glowing sun," sang the flower-maiden.

"The pink, rosy dawn and the glowing sun," a chorus of flowers replied.

"The wheel of the sun and its sweet light," chanted the flower-maiden with devotion.

"The wheel of the sun and its sweet light," the

chorus of flowers echoed with zeal.

"Beautiful chanting! I never knew dawn could be so glorious and sweet. Thank you!" Tom said cheerfully with a sense of release.

"You are most welcome," said the flower-maiden, who made a graceful bow.

Tom slowly inhaled the fresh morning air, smiling to himself as he spoke to the flower-maiden.

"Mostly, I have a hard time waking up early in the morning," Tom shared.

"Why is that?" she asked.

"I don't know. At times, the tail of the night, disguised as a caravan of dreams, holds me captive," said Tom in a hesitant voice.

"Recalling this glorious morning will set you free, you will see," said the flower-maiden, smiling.

"Brilliant! Now I get it; memory is like an alarm clock."

"Memory is like an alarm clock," the flower-maiden echoed after him. "Though less noisy and more effective," she added and lifted her leafy arms in an upward and jazzy motion.

"Wow, who are you?" Tom asked.

"My name is Seven," said the flower-maiden.

"What an unusual name," Tom said.

"Guess why," asked the flower-maiden.

Tom thought for a minute, and then began to speak:

"Today I have been to a most amazing maze.
I traveled about in seven and seventy ways
And met creatures of so many kinds and shapes.
I met Master Guardian 'Every-where'
And saw a hippo with a voracious appetite.
I spent some time with a talkative giraffe
And ran into a rude fly who buzzed a lot of fluff.
I conversed with a big, red cockroach
And befriended a monster shark.
And now, in the island of flowers,
I am ready to make a mark
With flowers by my side...or without."

"What a pretty poem," said the flower-maiden, her voice like gently chiming bells.

"What a colorful audience!" Tom said. "Thank you, flower-maiden, for sharing the magnificence of this garden with me. Who are you?" Tom asked again.

"My name is Seven," she answered again and placed her palms together close to her heart.

"I know, yet I wonder who you really are?"

"A flower-maiden in a Garden of Images I am. Some call me the Muse. Yes, I like to inspire and a-Muse!" Seven said, as she moved her crown petals up and down.

Tom looked amused and amazed.

"You are a fun muse to be with. Will I ever see you again?"

"Whenever you imagine loving light, first thing in the morning, know it is the seven rays of light brushing against your eyelids with rainbow tints and a butterfly kiss."

"Oh, my, I will always treasure this gift from your Garden of Images," said Tom. "Are you one of the subjects of this Kingdom of Monsters?" he asked, after a pause.

"Of course, I am," replied the flower-maiden.

"But you are so pretty!" Tom said in wonder.

"And who is it to say that monsters are ugly? One needs to know how to look," the flower-maiden replied in the sweetest voice.

"Quite so," said Tom in amazement. "Once, for instance, I thought all cockroaches ugly and scary. Now I know this is not so."

The flower-maiden picked two red apples from a nearby tree. "Why did I not meet you before, at the carnival, when the game 'Find the Dragon' began?" Tom asked.

"I am the surprise!" the flower-maiden said laughing and presenting Tom with a ripe, red apple. "I must confess, though, that I slept through the game."

"Slept? But why?" Tom wondered. "After

all, Dinosaur, the presidential monster himself, had invited all the subjects in this kingdom to participate in the game."

"The flowers sleep at night and awaken during the day," explained the flower-maiden brightly.

"That is in contradiction to the rules declared by Hippo at the start of the game! He said that all the monsters ought to be awake from the end of sunset to the start of sunrise."

"Every set of rules has an exception," the flower-maiden said. "We, the flowers, are the exception."

"Why?" Tom asked.

"Well, if all the monsters are awake at night and asleep during the day, someone must sleep through the night and tell the monsters how beautiful daytime can be."

"Too bad you missed the game."

"I played the game while being asleep," said the flower-maiden, smiling mysteriously.

"So it seems," Tom said, deep in thought. "My friend, the red cockroach Ear-El, says that we all play the game by our own rules."

By then, the night sky had begun to brighten. "Can you tell me where I can find the King of All Monsters," Tom asked the flower-maiden.

"Why do you need to find the king? Isn't this garden pretty enough?"

"Because I wish to play this game to the end," Tom replied.

"If this is so," said the pretty flower-maiden, "let me walk with you." The flower-maiden sprang out from where she was planted and stood up on the tip of her roots. "If you want me to walk you to the end of the game, you need to take off your bat costume," she advised.

"But," Tom protested, flapping his wings, "this is such a pretty disguise. It let me flee from the giant flies and soar high for fun in this magnificent palace!"

"This is how it works," explained the flower-maiden in her pleasant voice. "Toward the end of the game, all the monsters must take off their costumes. From now on, you are not going to need wings."

With much regret, Tom took off his bat outfit and put it between two flowerbeds. He looked at the costume and said, "When I first wore it, I thought it was a magnificent outfit, but now it seems like useless rags."

"All masks, even the most glorious, look dull before the break of dawn," said the flower-maiden. "Look, look!" she cried out in wonder.

When Tom looked in the direction she was pointing, he couldn't believe his eyes.

A snow-white bat emerged from where he had just dropped his costume. The bat spread his wings, took off, and vanished in the distance. Nothing remained of Tom's disguise.

"I have never seen a white bat before!"

"Nor have you ever been a bat. You put on a show just to play the game," the flower-maiden said. She took Tom's hand and led him to the green bridge at the edge of the garden. "Cross this bridge and continue to walk straight ahead," she said.

"And the apple?"

"This apple is your endgame," said the flower-maiden and turned around, preparing to leave him.

"Is this your endgame goodbye, or is this the end of our friendship?"

"No, it is just the beginning," said Seven and tilted her body gently toward Tom. She opened her rainbow fan, swung it rapidly, and blew the scented air of the garden onto Tom's face. Tom closed his eyes, trying to preserve the sensation.

"First thing in the morning," Seven said, "when you feel a gentle breeze on your eyelashes, remember the seven rays of the sun and know that my rainbow fan is not too far away."

"Thank you. I have learned so many things through this game," Tom said and took a bite of the apple in his hand. "I have never met a pretty flower-maiden like you before," he said.

"You will again, if you only learn how to look," whispered the flower-maiden. She closed her colorful petals one by one, lifted herself gently onto the edge of her roots, and tiptoed out of sight.

Goodbye...
Hello, sweet dreams

CHAPTER 17

After All, It Was Just a Game

Another corridor awaited Tom beyond the bridge. This one was white, sparkling, and bright. Tom walked alongside the long, whiter-than-white walls, arriving at the doorway of a round room, which was equally white and bright, but empty and windowless. Only a wide, round chimney extended down from the center of the ceiling. The air inside was still.

How could I possibly climb up that chimney?

Tom decided to wait. He waited and waited and waited some more, until his eyes closed.

He remembered his new friends, Jack the shark, Ear-El the red cockroach, and Seven the flower-maiden. To his amazement, he felt that he was ascending effortlessly up the round chimney, which gradually turned into a long, transparent glass cylinder. Tom could now see the different passages and hallways of the Temple of Puzzles and Puzzlement.

I could never have imagined that this maze would be so vast and elaborate.

He then noticed the various monsters dashing back and forth along the corridors.

"How funny you are, my favorite monsters," he giggled, beaming with joy.

There was Hippo, having fun strolling while licking yellow ice cream out of a large, green cone. A family of greedy flies followed him. Each fly carried a small cone of ice cream, the dessert treats from Hippo's feast.

"At last, the flies get to enjoy a hearty meal!" Tom laughed heartily.

And there was Gurgle, the talkative giraffe. On his right stood his cousin, the wild boar, and to his left his good pal, Rhino. The excited motion of Gurgle's head and neck made clear the giraffe was in the midst of telling yet another amazing ostrich tale.

"How ridiculous and funny you are, my lovely monsters!"

Jack the Shark was parked in the corner, his big mouth wide open. Out of it came the many-legged caterpillar.

Tom's felt more and more elated at the thought that he might, at last, reach his destination. He felt lighter and lighter, as if the force of gravity had deserted him, and not surprised when he ascended faster and faster up the transparent glass cylinder.

Looking out, Tom noticed his friend, the Royal Guardian Every-where, holding a sign: "Wherever you are, there you are!"

The wind howled in Tom's ears as he sped upward on his journey. He could not quite hear what Every-where was saying. But, reading his lips, he guessed that Every-where was trying to tell him that the King of All Monsters was right up there.

"Where is my friend Ear-El?" he wondered aloud, searching the crowd. "He must be busy figuring things out."

Tom sped upward faster and faster. He imagined that the top floor would be the most amazing of all.

So many wonderful surprises have come my way so far. I wonder how much better it could get when I arrive at the palace of his Majesty, the King of All Monsters.

Suddenly, the howling wind was deafening, and Tom closed his eyes.

When he opened his eyes again, he discovered, to his utmost surprise, that he was standing in the vast and deserted graveyard of machines.

In the distance, at the edge of the graveyard, a mysterious, tall figure smoked a pipe. The billowing smoke resembled ghost-like clouds, spiraling up like a feathered snake or a dragon dancing under the dim light of a street lamp.

Tom ran toward the mysterious figure and

blurted out impatiently, "Are you the King of All Monsters?"

The figure took the pipe out of its mouth and roared in laughter.

"Why are you laughing?"

"Is your name Tom Perry?" asked the mysterious figure.

"Yes, that is my name. How did you guess?" At that very moment, Tom realized that he was talking to a policeman.

"We have been looking all over for you since early afternoon. And if you insist on calling me 'The King of All Monsters,' go ahead, I don't mind," said the police officer in a kindly tone, laughing again.

Out of nowhere, three more policemen with sniffing dogs appeared.

"Is it him?" inquired an officer who seemed to be in charge, pointing at Tom.

"Yes, it is," answered the pipe-smoking policeman. "The boy must have fallen asleep under an old car, and because he was cold and hungry, he had a strange dream. When he woke up, he asked me an odd question."

"What was it?" inquired the higher-ranked officer.

"What did he ask?" asked the other policemen.

The dogs wagged their tails.

"Never mind," said the pipe-smoking officer, waving his hand and smiling warmly at Tom. "It's getting very late. We had better get him home."

"Home, definitely home," Tom said, while riding in the police car. "I was lost in a caravan of dreams. But now that I found my way back, I am suddenly awakened."

Tom's parents, worried and concerned, were waiting at the entrance to their house.

"Good evening," said his father, looking a bit grim.

"Good evening, Dad," Tom said, turning his gaze to his mom. "So good to be back!"

"Welcome home, child," his mother said and hugged her "lost and found" son. "We were worried sick about you!" she added while walking with him inside the house.

In the dining room, the table was set for dinner.

"What do you have to say in your defense?" asked his father when he and Tom took their seats. "I'm listening!"

Tom's mother placed fresh, home-baked food on the table.

Tom felt uneasy and hesitant, but the enticing aroma of his mom's cooking made him feel at home, and his mood lifted.

"I am so sorry for giving you and Mom so

much grief," he said, "and I regret it very much. But I must say that, now, after all I have been through, I feel like a changed boy, as if something within me has finally awakened!"

"Good morning and happy awakening!" said his dad, his grin turning into a smile. "Or perhaps we should say good night?"

"Forgive me, Dad, for what I did to the alarm clocks. It was foolish and hasty. Tomorrow morning, I promise to wake up on my own," Tom declared as he finished a whole plate of eggplant blintzes, his favorite dish.

"You are forgiven," said his dad and passed a slice of bread to Tom. "Help yourself, please, and don't forget to pick up the signed letter for your schoolteacher tomorrow."

"Thanks, Dad," said Tom, pausing momentarily while pouring a cup of hot chocolate. "By the way, I hope that the poor alarm clocks have been restored to health by now. Have they?"

"Doing very poorly, I'm afraid," said his father, leafing through the newspaper. "I did my best to mend them, but to no avail."

"Too bad, Dad," said Tom. "What is there to be done with broken clocks?"

"Next Sunday, we are going to take a walk to a special cemetery for machines, where we will bury them in the proper, ceremonial way," said father half-seriously, half-jokingly, while pretending to read his newspaper.

"A cemetery for machines?" Tom raised his head and looked at his father, who slowly lowered the newspaper and finally put it aside. Their eyes met. After a brief silence, Tom continued: "That's a great idea! While I was there, I saw many kinds of machines, big and small, and various types of cars. As to clocks, especially the old-fashioned ones, I don't recall seeing very many."

"Really?" Father raised his eyebrows. "When were you there?"

"This afternoon," said Tom. "I found new friends to play with and visited Ian and his family. They live in a big yellow bus with a chimney on top."

"New friends?" Father was taken by surprise.

"Yes, Ian, my new friend, and his pals are my playmates now," Tom replied. Feeling elated, he went on to say, "Ian's dad sang a song for us kids about Vasco da Gama, the great explorer who was the first to sail all the way from Portugal to Asia."

"I'm delighted to hear that while being away from school you have managed to learn something new!" exclaimed his father.

"Oh yes, I did. I also saw a dream catcher at Ian's. And Mel, Ian's mom, told us how this charming object came to be in her possession; it traveled all the way from New Amsterdam."

"I know how to catch fish with a net, but I had no idea there was one for dreams!" his dad responded with surprise. "There is a big and interesting world out there. What else did you learn?"

"So much more, but it's a long story. I'll tell you more on Sunday, at the funeral for our poor alarm clocks."

"Good night, then," said his father and kissed him. "Tonight, I am not going to set up any alarm clocks."

"Good night," said Tom, smiling, as he retired to his room.

Early next morning, dense light streamed through the blinds, like honey sliding on thin rays. Tom felt the sweetness of the light on his closed eyelids.

No alarm clocks rang.

But Tom woke up at fifteen minutes before seven o'clock. "It feels so much better without those noisy clocks." He yawned and brushed his teeth.

Mother was setting up the dining table for

breakfast. When Tom, all washed and groomed, was seated, she asked, "Where were you really yesterday?"

"I visited the kingdom of the lovely monsters," replied Tom, deep in thought as he sipped his milk.

"The kingdom of monsters! Well, well, my boy, you are my kind of lovely monster, yourself." Mother laughed and kissed Tom on his forehead. "And what exactly did you do there?"

"I participated in a game, hoping to win the title of The Most Monstrous Monster in the Kingdom of Monsters."

Mother opened her mouth in disbelief.

"Don't take it so seriously, Mom. It was just a game!"

The end is another beginning.

Acknowledgments

Special thanks to the editors: Madeline Stone, Miron Baron, and John Mailing of AuthorU.org.

Copyediting and proofreading by Self-Publishing Services Inc. Much gratitude to Catharine Clarke for final line editing and management of print production.

The help and encouragement of Judith Briles of AuthorU.org are gratefully acknowledged.

Thanks to Dr. Laura Singer-Magdoff, Ed.D. for inspirational guidance, and to Soomee Elissa Lubin for assistance with the initial process.

About the Author

C**armela Tal Baron** is the author of the award-winning story, ***Down the Monster Hole*** or ***Don't Be Afraid, I Am Only a Child***, a book for children and the young at heart. A Denver public librarian, who was one of the judges in the AuthorU.org 2016 literary contest, wrote in her laudatory report: "Even children who don't tend to read many books will be attracted to read this one." A shorter version of this book, in Hebrew, won distinction as one of the ten best children's books published in Israel in 1971 (Sifriat Poalim, Tel Aviv).

Carmela Tal Baron is a New York-based poet, writer, and songwriter-vocalist whose background is in visual arts and design. She is the founding director of Designs for Enlightenment - Turtle Island. Its products include books; CDs; videos; digital prints and 3-D designs; fine art (paintings, drawings, collages, and photography); interior and environmental design; art installations, and Art as Tools for Peace.

How To Order

Down the Monster Hole or ***Don't Be Afraid, I'm Ony a Child***
is available from Amazon, Barnes & Noble, and all major online
retailers. Bookstore orders can be placed directly through Ingram
Content Group at www.ingramcontent.com

CPSIA information can be obtained
at www.ICGtesting.com
Printed in the USA
BVHW062105110619
550738BV00011B/17/P